"I can't believe [...] you want me to stay."

As if in answer, an implacable hardness entered Leo's eyes. "No. But my son does. And he thinks he already has plenty of reasons to hate me."

"So you're going to make me stay until—"

"Until you show your true colors."

"Maybe it's you who can't see me as I really am," Gina snapped. "You're going to use me to get close to your son!" She drew a breath. "What kind of father have you been that he should hate you?"

The answer was long in coming. "Thanks to his mother, no kind of father at all. Dom has only been living with me for six months."

Some of Gina's harsh preconceptions of Leo Sterne shattered. Had his ex-wife died? Or remarried? Curiosity was the first step to caring. Gina was already curious—and close to caring about the resolve of this father-son conflict.

SUSAN NAPIER was born on Valentine's Day, so perhaps it is only fitting that she should become a romance writer. She started out as a reporter for New Zealand's largest evening newspaper before resigning to marry the paper's chief reporter. After the birth of their two children she did some freelancing for a film production company and then settled down to write her first romance. "Now," she says, "I am in the enviable position of being able to build my career around my home and family."

HARLEQUIN PRESENTS
885—SWEET AS MY REVENGE
924—THE COUNTERFEIT SECRETARY

HARLEQUIN ROMANCE
2711—LOVE IN THE VALLEY
2723—SWEET VIXEN

These books may be available at your local bookseller.

Don't miss any of our special offers. Write to us at the following address for information on our newest releases.

Harlequin Reader Service
901 Fuhrmann Blvd., P.O. Box 1397, Buffalo, NY 14240
Canadian address: P.O. Box 603,
Fort Erie, Ont. L2A 9Z9

SUSAN NAPIER

the lonely season

Harlequin Books

TORONTO • NEW YORK • LONDON
AMSTERDAM • PARIS • SYDNEY • HAMBURG
STOCKHOLM • ATHENS • TOKYO • MILAN

The lonely season in lonely lands, when fled
And half the birds, and mists lie low, and the sun
Is rarely seen, nor strayeth far from his bed;
the short days pass unwelcomed one by one.

(Robert Bridges)

Harlequin Presents first edition December 1986
ISBN 0-373-10940-7

Original hardcover edition published in 1986
by Mills & Boon Limited

CHAPTER ONE

'DAMNIT, Peter, this is the first and last time. I don't know why I let you talk me into it!'

Peter Knight came up behind the tall, shadowed figure and looked out of the window at the knots of laughing house-guests gathered around the long food and drink-laden tables in the marble courtyard. There were twenty of them, drinking champagne and eating barbecued seafood, and none of them seemed to notice that their host was not among them.

'You had other things on your mind, as I recall,' Peter commented quietly. 'And at the time you thought it might be a good way of killing two birds with one stone.'

'Well, I was wrong,' came the answering growl from the darkness. Ice clinked against Italian crystal as a glass was raised and lowered and the voice continued, flavoured with contempt, 'Paradise is wasted on this lot. I may not spend much time here but when I do it's because this is as close to tranquillity as I'll ever get. I doubt if that bunch of freeloaders down there even understands what the word means.'

'*Useful* freeloaders, though. And they'll be gone tomorrow so you'll have your tranquillity back again.'

'Except I won't be here to enjoy it.' Leonard Sterne turned abruptly from the balcony and caught sight of his employee's face. 'It's all right, Peter, I understand the necessity even if I don't appreciate it. But next time we want to grease the wheels of commerce, let's just hire a charter yacht for a weekend cruise.'

'The only reason *they're* here, is because you're here. A yacht would still have been no use if you weren't aboard.'

'I had no choice but to come, Peter.' The tawny-coloured eyes glinted with frustration and impatience as Leonard Sterne contemplated the reason for his trip to Paradise Island two weeks ahead of schedule. 'Damn Miss Hamilton, what a hell of a time for her to break a leg!' He began to prowl back and forth in the long, spare, beautiful room that acted as both office and bedroom, conscious of his secretary's silent sympathy and grateful to him for not expressing it. Pity was the last thing he needed.

'What are you going to do?'

'Nothing. Not yet, anyway. Miss Hamilton says she can cope with the lessons and this agency woman we brought over can cope with general supervision. As soon as Miss Hamilton is back on her feet we can go back to the original arrangement.'

'And you?'

'What about me?' The snarl shot out before he could stop it and he followed it up just as quickly. 'I'm sorry, Peter, I'm tired so make allowances for me, will you.'

The apology was unnecessary. Peter knew well the strain that Leo was under. In the ten years Peter had worked for him he had rarely known Leo to take a holiday. He had worked hard and, until recently, played just as hard. In the past six months, however, he had been confronted with a totally new series of problems that couldn't be solved by intelligence, determination and planning. Instead, the answer lay in qualities that Leo had never cultivated: gentleness, patience, kindness. In typical fashion Leo had made his decision. If the solution to his problems lay in making a fundamental change to his lifestyle he would do it. Peter wondered whether it had occurred to him that he might fail. It must have done, for Leo always considered all the angles, but this time he hadn't even mentioned the possibility. Perhaps because this time, for the first time, it mattered deeply, emotionally, that he succeed.

'I only meant to ask whether this means any other change of plan,' Peter said mildly.

'No. Dominic has to start to accept me . . . and I him. That's not going to happen if we keep letting circumstances intervene. I'll be back two weeks from today.'

'And how are *you* going to cope?' Peter asked drily, adding, as he saw the dangerous expression, 'I mean, with all that free time?'

Leo's mouth twisted sardoncially. 'Perhaps I'll find I like it. You might have trouble digging me out of here when the month is up.'

Peter grinned. 'I doubt that very much. You can't change the habits of a lifetime in a few weeks. Even tranquillity has its limits. I don't think you were cut out to permanently inhabit paradise.'

'More likely the other place.' Leo Sterne gave a harsh laugh. 'Just make sure you keep me in touch.'

'I wouldn't dare otherwise,' Peter replied, finishing his own drink. 'Although you have a good man in John Standish. Have you decided yet whether you'll let him keep the position permanently?'

'Not yet.' Leo set his glass down abruptly and threw his head back aggressively, squaring the breadth of his shoulders as he did so, the King of the jungle, defending his turf. 'Time enough for that when I see how things go with Dominic.'

Peter shrugged his acceptance, not pushing the point, though they both knew the decision would have to come soon. In any other man he might have said that the hesitation denoted a lack of confidence, but Leo was the most self-confident man he knew. No doubt he had good reason for the delay.

A burst of laughter drifted up over the concrete parapet and Leo ran a splayed hand through the thick, dark blond hair. 'God, I'm tired. I think I'll go down for a swim. It might clear my head.' He jerked his head towards the raucous sounds below. 'They're having too good a time to miss me.'

'You want me to come along?'

The blond head shifted negatively. 'I'm not drunk, Peter. And the lagoon's shallow. But do me a favour and head off anyone who suggests a swim. I'll only be half an hour.'

Leo didn't even bother to pick up a towel. He took one of the back exits and strode through the darkened undergrowth towards the low hiss of the sea. His stamina must have suffered over the past six months. At one time he could party until dawn, put in a full day's work and repeat the process all over again. These days there was no time for empty social games, he was working twenty hours out of twenty-four. In two weeks that would change and at last he would be able to direct all his energies towards a single purpose: Dominic. It was for his son that he was shedding many of his responsibilities, determined that from now on the boy would have a reasonably normal and secure family life.

Leo frowned as he recalled Peter's question about John Standish. It had probed a hidden sore spot. What would happen if he could not adjust to this new, less demanding life? Power was like a drug; was he sufficiently committed to Dominic to reject its seductive pull? Of course, it wasn't as if he was completely retiring, at thirty-five he wasn't ready to do that, he would still be involved in the day-to-day running of the publishing part of his business, but that was very different from the hectic jet-setting of the past decade. From now on he planned to be based almost entirely in New Zealand.

There was also the question of whether he was equal to this challenge he had presented himself with. Leo was accustomed to controlling people and situations with a word but he couldn't do that with Dominic. There was no easy way, the damage was too deep and too lasting ... thanks to Cynthia's selfishness—and his own. Now it was for Dominic to set the pace, and Leo to follow.

He must try to recapture some of his own long-lost innocence in order to meet the boy on his own terms. And they would be hard ones. He knew from bitter experience that Dom had an extraordinary—some might say inherited—stubbornness. He also stocked an arsenal of emotional weapons that he didn't even know he possessed, thank God. So far he had barely acknowledged the presence of his father in his life, which wasn't surprising considering the schedule that Leo had been keeping. But he knew that the reason for Dom's refusal to even say his name was far more basic. If Dom would only *look* at him, with something other than that shuttered or accusing stare . . . There were six years of fathering to make up, but he couldn't even start until Dom was willing to let him.

Leo swore under his breath as he arrived at the beach and saw that a couple were already swimming. He turned and plunged back through the trees. He'd go over the ridge to the next bay. It was less accessible and thus less popular with visitors to Paradise Villa. Up until now he had only invited personal friends—and lovers—to the island, never realising how much he had come to rely on it as an occasional bolt-hole. He had surprised himself with the strength of his resentment of the people who now polluted its peace with their revelry. Had he surprised Peter too? It was difficult to tell. The quiet, unassuming young man was not easy to read, yet he had a knack of anticipating Leo's demands. He'd probably already investigated several alternative exotic locations to impress the many contacts it was necessary to maintain in the world of international publishing.

Leo reached the beach in a leisurely twenty minutes, and began to strip off his clothes. There was something cleansing about swimming in the raw. For the most part Leo enjoyed living a sophisticated life but there were times when he felt the need to shrug off the mantle of civilisation and reaffirm his elemental self. Here on

Paradise he could reassure himself that he still existed, separate from the luxurious world he had created for himself to inhabit.

He was about to step out from the inky shadows of the palms when he heard a splash from the lagoon. Damn! Had someone swum around the point? He paused, fighting frustration. Had someone seen him on the track? There were two unattached women in the party who had made no secret of their interest. Both were attractive but Leo had found their attempts at flirtation irritating rather than arousing. This conflict with Dominic was even affecting his libido!

Then he saw her, rising from the shallows of the lagoon like a sleek, brown Aphrodite. It was a young girl, wearing a pareu that clung to her lush curves like the touch of a lover. Her hair was long and dark, spread wetly over her bare, brown shoulders. She must be from the village, but why was she on this side of the island? Come to meet a lover perhaps? Leo relaxed and smiled in the darkness. Or had she been curious about the visitors and come to satisfy her curiosity?

He watched as she lifted the hem of the pareu away from her thighs and the moonlight gilded long, beautiful legs. Her wrists flexed as she wrung out the fabric and then straightened to slick the tail of wet hair between her shoulder blades. Leo wished she would turn in his direction so that he could see her face, see if it matched the lovely body. His senses stirred as she lifted her profile to the sky and raised her hands to squeeze the wet tail hanging down her back. Her full, round breasts rose too, outlined by the wet fabric enfolding them. A real beauty in a rare setting. He thought of the made-up and manicured women back at the villa. He much preferred this innocent, unadorned naturalness. Though perhaps, not so innocent. She was fully developed, and women married young in this part of the world. Leo felt his pulse quicken and savoured the sensation. Perhaps his libido wasn't as depressed as he had thought. He stepped forward, just as a mass of cloud swallowed the moon.

'You're trespassing. Did you know that?'

Gina spun at the first sound, drawing a quick breath of fear.

'Don't be afraid. I'm not going to hurt you.'

The soothing words had the opposite effect to what the speaker intended. Gina's fear turned to shock and then horror as she recognised the voice. *Leonard Sterne.* Here, on her blessed island of retreat, just when she had lulled herself into believing that, this time, things might turn out as she wanted them to. Oh, *damn.* She should have realised that the plane she saw coming over had meant more than just supplies, but she hadn't wanted her peace disturbed by unwelcome apprehensions. So she had gone on as usual, come around to the bay for the last swim of the day as she had every evening for two weeks.

The warm salt water chilled on her exposed skin as she relived the humiliation of her first, and last, meeting with Leonard Sterne. If he recognised her now she would be humiliated all over again.

Panicking she whirled and began to run along the beach, through the shallows, towards the safety of the trees at the far end of the sand. As soon as she heard his laugh she knew she had made a mistake. It was too dark for him to see her face, she could have brazened it out. After all, he had never heard *her* voice. Fear lent wings to her feet as she splashed free of the water. If only she could have dived back into the lagoon and swum around the point back to her own beach, but her espadrilles were lying up in the grass somewhere and the seabed beyond the point was composed of razor-sharp coral and harboured a few of the ocean's most poisonous inhabitants. She never went swimming straight out from the bungalow unless her feet were protected and not even to escape the devil himself was she willing to risk it tonight.

Gasping for breath, aware of the long legs gaining, Gina nearly ran into the coconut palm which had fallen across the sand, its fronds dipping lazily into the water. It took her a precious few seconds to scramble over it, whereas her pursuer vaulted it with ease and caught at the fluttering edge of her wet pareu.

She fell and he fell with her. Gina's hands shot out automatically to push him away and she choked on another stunned gasp as she wrenched them back. He was naked! His body was hot in contrast to her cool, damp one, so that she felt his steamy impression with every pore.

'Hey, calm down, I'm not going to hurt you,' he muttered but it wasn't his words that stopped her struggle. His gentle wrestling was making her more than ever aware of his nakedness and she was appalled to realise that intermingled with her fear was an astonished acknowledgment of his powerful masculinity. He was breathing as hard as she was, his chest pressing against her breasts as he filled his lungs with warm night air.

Gina willed her trembling limbs to stillness as he murmured something in Fijian. He thought she was a local girl! If she hadn't aroused his hunting instinct by fleeing she probably could have escaped with a few polite phrases. Now she sensed that more than just his hunting instinct was aroused. She could feel the hot stirring of his body against her thigh and trembled anew. She should never have let Daniel persuade her to come to this island but she had been too shattered by events to put up much resistance. And now, here she was, trapped in the arms of a man who had been witness to the moment of her shame and disillusionment.

'Who are you? Where do you come from? The village?' His voice was as warmly enveloping as the darkness and Gina had to clench her teeth to resist its allure.

He laughed softly against her jaw. 'Not talking? Shy? Or just preserving your anonymity? I know you must speak English. All the villagers do.'

Gina opened her mouth but even before she tried to speak she knew that no sound would come out. The familiar, hated ache was in her throat, the feeling of thickness, the hard obstruction of bone and sinew that haunted her nightmares. All she could manage was a faint, rasping moan.

'There's a penalty I extract from lovely trespassers like you.' Panic made her start to struggle again and the satiny strength of his arms tightened around her as he warned on a liquid note of laughter, 'Don't do that, sweetheart, at the moment I'm rather vulnerable to every soft ripple of your skin. I might be tempted to do more than just take a kiss.'

She felt the truth of his statement against her hip and gave a gasp as she tried to wriggle away. He pressed closer, rolling on to his side and taking her with him. His heart beat strongly against the arms she had crossed defensively over her almost naked breasts. She felt his breath against her cheek, her mouth, and stiffened.

'Ssshhh, one kiss, is that so much to ask for the price of a swim?' He nuzzled the side of her mouth and the scent of rum filled Gina's nostrils. He had been drinking, she realised with a stab of relief, and was just having an uninhibited little game with an unknown female. As long as the moon stayed in hiding she was safe. And she couldn't say that there wasn't a certain vengeful satisfaction in having Leonard Sterne pleading for a kiss from the despised Virginia Bennett. He had thought her a cheap little tramp, a wrecker of marriages, had implied with his contempt that he would never soil himself with her kind of woman. How self-righteous he had been; and how terribly, terribly wrong.

He was no longer holding her as tightly, and Gina told herself that she should get away, now, but her limbs felt strangely heavy. The hand that had clamped on to her shoulder now slid under her body to cup her shoulder-blade and scoop her into his roughly-haired chest, the other tilting her chin to align their mouths. His lips were amazingly warm and tender and Gina's heart began to thud. She had been kissed rarely enough for it to be still something of a novelty and she couldn't help comparing this exploratory sensuality with the hard yet oddly unsatisfying kisses that she had been given by the man she had loved, and who she thought had loved her. But of course he hadn't loved her, only used her, and although she hadn't known it at the time perhaps her womanhood had sensed it and that's why Niven's kisses hadn't aroused her more than they did. At least Leonard Sterne was kissing her because he *wanted* to, not as part of some sordid charade, not because he pitied her, or wondered what it was like to kiss a freak. He wasn't kissing her to set her up for a fall. He was doing it because he was a man and she was a woman and in the darkness Gina let herself respond.

He was deliciously skilled. Gina opened her eyes wide and stared into the blackness above his head as a variety of odd sensations began to chase under her skin. Her defensively crossed hands clutched on to the bare hunch of shoulders above her as his lips parted to move the delicate moisture of his tongue against the firm line of her mouth. He softened her lips with unhurried ease until she relaxed enough to let him inside. But the single plunge of his tongue into the spicy depths sent such a shaft of pleasure through her that Gina took fright. She squirmed but Leo misinterpreted her efforts to get away. He slid his powerful thighs against the thin barrier of her pareu, lifting his head to ask huskily,

'You like that, hmmm? Is this what you came looking for on my beach?' She caught the gleam of his eyes in the darkness, like the glint of a wild animal's, the mane of hair tousled by the chase giving him an even more predatory appearance. Desperately Gina tried to force out a single word—*no*—but her tongue was clumsy in her mouth as if, somehow, he had enmeshed it in a sensual spell.

His head swooped again and Gina's senses went into

a state of shock as she felt the moist intimacy of his tongue against hers. She curled her tongue sharply away but he followed with a stabbing thrust that impaled her helplessly beneath him. His initial playfulness was dissolving into something deeper and more dangerous and Gina trembled as the muscles in his arms and legs tightened involuntarily against her, his chest shifting over hers, his hips flexing. For all her inexperience she recognised the driving sexual tension that had entered his body and was rapidly infecting hers. She felt his hand upon her breast, discovering the pebble-hardness of her nipple against his palm and tore her mouth away, managing a ragged croak which descended into a cracked moan as his face dipped to rub with gentle abrasiveness across the skin swelling above the damp fabric. His teeth tested the resilience of her flesh, then moved up to her throat, where he paused at the first ridge of scars.

'What . . .?'

His recoil was like a kick in the teeth. With all her strength Gina tore away and ran blindly into the trees, hating him, her pain giving her impetus to escape. She heard him follow her into the whispering bush, his voice calling, husky with a combination of amusement and desire. After a muffled thud and curse his voice sounded distinctly less amused and Gina crouched in the midst of a clump of prickly ferns, her heart pounding furiously.

When his voice faded, violent reaction set in and slow, hot tears began to squeeze from her tightly closed eyes. She didn't want to cry. She thought she had used up her quota of tears long ago, and hated herself for her weakness, but still they came. Inside her there was relief and anger and a kind of guilty excitement churning around, making her feel sick. It had come as a shock to realise how vulnerable she was, despite her experience with Niven. It was only when Leonard Sterne had touched her scars that she had come to her senses. The scars were an ugly reminder that men were selfish, shallow, deceitful . . . and so practised in deception that they were quite capable of blinding themselves to their own cruelty. She was just another stray, grey cat to Leonard Sterne back there in the darkness. He could have taken her on the sand, not knowing or caring about her innocence or lack of it, and walked away afterwards without an ounce of remorse. That's the way men were made.

Shame raked over her as Gina reminded herself that the naked man whom she had let touch her so intimately was the *reason* for her lonely misery of the last eight months, the reason that she had needed to be bullied into coming here. If it hadn't been for Leonard Sterne, Niven would never have been driven to such incredible lengths to obtain his freedom.

She froze at a nearby sound. Had he come back? Slowly, fearfully, she opened her eyes and found herself staring at a young boy. The moon had cleared, and by the chinks of light filtering through the trees Gina could see that he was very brown and thin, dressed only in ragged shorts and sneakers. His hair was dark and brushed his shoulders and his eyes under pleated brows were also dark. What was he doing out so late? Had he seen what had happened on the beach? What had so nearly happened? Looking closely Gina realised that she had seen him before, at a distance, collecting shells on the beach. Perhaps he belonged to one of the couples who worked at the villa.

Gina wiped at her tears, unaware that to the boy she looked almost like a child herself . . . uncertain, afraid. A kindred spirit. Someone else who had been hurt by *that man*.

Gina held her breath, wondering if the boy was going to betray her to his parents' employer. She smiled tentatively, but he didn't return the gesture. Instead he held out something . . . her shoes. So he *had* seen. Gina wanted to thank him but she was afraid that the sound of her strange voice might frighten him so instead she mimed her appreciation. It was as if she had hit him. His face took on a pinched, hurt look, and he melted back into the trees leaving her alone, confounded by his behaviour.

It took her twenty minutes to find her way back to the path that led around the series of stony outcrops to the small, whitewashed wooden bungalow that was her home for a month. She went around, flicking on all the lights to reassure herself that she really was alone, and then flicked them all off and sat in the dark in the small room that she used as a work-room. She usually worked after her nightly swim ... or pretended to work. Daniel would be furious with her if he knew just how little she had achieved so far. But she still felt drained, empty of inspiration and deathly afraid of trying, and failing.

It had been her lack of inspiration that had got her sent here in the first place. Daniel Austin was more than just the editor of the children's books that Gina illustrated, he was a friend, an adviser, the man who had encouraged her in her fumblings towards a career against all the odds.

'But *illustrating*!' Margaret Bennett had shrieked when her youngest daughter had taken up her pen in return for a contract. 'It's so commercial, darling! If you must dabble why can't you produce some real art, instead of those wretched little childish things? I know you have your problems, Virginia, but poverty isn't one of them. How can I tell my friends that you're actually *working* for a living? It reflects back on me, you know.'

It hadn't, partly because her mother never mentioned that her daughter Virginia was actually Gina Bennett, illustrator, and partly because none of her friends ever showed any interest in the youngest of the three Bennett girls ... too awkward, too embarrassing. In the Bennetts' social circles it was unacceptable to be handicapped. One could have nervous breakdowns or suffer infectious social diseases, but Gina's presence had been tolerated only because her particular affliction meant that she could be safely and easily treated as if she didn't exist.

But for Daniel she had existed. He had helped her build her talent, and her sense of purpose and self-worth, and had always been honest with her.

'You're a mess,' he had told her brutally, four weeks ago in his office. 'And so are these drawings. I wouldn't submit them to a kindergarten. The deadline is in another six weeks; if you don't pull your finger out soon you're not only going to jeopardise your contract, you're going to let down a very fine writer who trusted you to do justice to his story.'

Gina had stared out of his office window at the dreary autumn rain sheeting against the glass. 'Sorry, Daniel, but I just don't seem to be able to get my teeth into this one,' she whispered.

'You liked *Jao and The Magician* when you first read it. You had all sorts of ideas. What happened?'

Gina shrugged and Daniel gave a snort. 'OK, don't tell me, but don't think I'm going to let you get away with ruining this reputation that we've built up for you. You're going to deliver that book on schedule if I have to beat it out of you. But I don't think I'll have to.' His harried face crinkled into a smile. 'I have the perfect place for you. Away from all this dank, dark weather and that interfering mother of yours. A tropical island paradise, just the kind that Jao's Magician might inhabit. What do you say?'

Gina's dark brows remained rumpled though she couldn't deny the idea was tempting. Auckland's winters were mild compared to some, but it had been wet and windy for weeks and the specialist had told Gina to beware of colds and influenza until the healing was complete. Consequently she had been cooped up even more than usual and prey to more than usual of her 'interfering' mother's complaints and suggestions about her future.

'Where is this island?' she husked, resisting the urge to cover her mouth with her hand. Daniel, at least, had always accepted her for what she was.

'Somewhere near Fiji, don't ask me exactly where, it's only a dot in the Pacific, but it's warm and dry, and there'll be nothing to distract or bother you other than nature herself in all her primitive beauty.'

'You want to maroon me on an uninhabited island?' Gina grimaced. 'Am I really that desperate?'

'It's not uninhabited, and *I'm* that desperate to drag you out of that hole you seem to have got into. Look, Gina, trust me, it's just what you need. There's one village there but most of the island is privately owned and the bungalow you'll be in rates as some kind of tax write-off. The owner has a publishing company and they shunt authors with problems out there away from all the temptations of civilisation. The accommodation is sound, there's running water and electricity, and a full stock of stores. What more could you ask?'

'A reason. How come *I'm* offered this magnificent opportunity?' Gina asked sarcastically, suspecting his answer as she watched him scratch at his grizzled head.

'Because this publishing company is the one that's going to publish your new book. *The Long Silence*. How are the revisions going, by the way?'

Gina evaded his gaze and he sighed. 'I thought so. You haven't even looked at them, have you, Gina?'

'I really don't know that I want it published,' she muttered defensively.

'Bull!' he challenged her. 'Why expend all that time and effort writing a full-length book if you never intended it to see the light of day? Why show it to me? Why not chuck it straight in the bin? Because you knew it was good, that's why. Because you *wanted* me to bully you into not wasting a gutsy talent, *that's* why!'

'It was an impulse,' Gina denied with a shrug, 'a fluke. I have enough problems at the moment with my drawing without having to worry about re-working my deathless prose.'

'It's not deathless and you know it,' Daniel said quietly. 'Sure it's raw and badly structured but it has a power and potential that book editors dream about. And I'm not about to let you hide behind your illustrating work as an excuse for not finishing this book.'

'I'm not hiding. But you said yourself that those are a mess,' she gestured towards the folio on his desk.

'Are you sure you're not subconsciously blocking yourself to avoid the *real* issue?'

'Blocking myself?' Gina rasped angrily. 'Daniel, you know how much my talent matters to me. It's been my lifeline! How can you even think that I might deliberately try to fail?'

'I didn't say it was deliberate. I'm just pointing out that once you've finished this Jao book then you have no reason *not* to do those revisions for me. I know it must be painful for you.'

'What? Manipulating characters in a work of fiction?'

Daniel smiled with a gentleness that gave his forty-year-old face a childlike sweetness. He could be crude, he could be brutal, he could be deflating, but he could also see through brick walls.

'Gina, why do you think I pressed you to use this Borelli pen-name? Because I know how threatened this book makes you feel, and I know that in spite of everything you really don't want to hurt anyone. If you want to call autobiography fiction that's fine—as far as the rest of the world is concerned. But I like to call a spade a spade.'

Gina had never told him about Niven, she never talked about him to anyone. How had he guessed? The question was in her dark eyes.

'Gina, honey, eight months ago you were on top of the world, nothing daunted you, you told me that you had suddenly realised that the only real handicap in your life was the one you gave yourself. You were like a bud in flower. And then, overnight, the flower wilts. You can't work, you lose your confidence, you start acting like you're some kind of freak and then you have this operation and go completely to pieces, just when your wildest dreams are finally realised. Why?—I asked myself. Where did my lovely, lively Gina go? And then you march in one morning, looking as if you've come out of the business end of a meat-grinder and lay a manuscript on me that rips my guts out. It's got power, Gina, because it has so much truth in it, so much of *you*.'

It had everything of her. After she had written it she had felt squeezed dry of all feeling, able to cope with life only by taking it day by day. What she had hoped would be a catharsis for her had instead only been the first step to healing. And it hurt; so much that she shut herself off from everything and everyone. Maybe it would be good to get away, but at what cost? She could hardly bring herself to even read Daniel's criticisms of her book, let alone act on them. How did one re-structure truth? She had written what had happened, the culmination of four years of silent frustration and unspoken pain, of loneliness, of despair, of hopes won and lost and of the final bitter betrayal.

'Grasp the nettle, Gina,' Daniel urged her softly. 'Go out to this island and find yourself again. You can't hide forever. And stop being so bloody self-conscious. Take your hand away from your mouth. You know, after a few months' practising with that new voice of yours you'll be knocking 'em dead. That gravelly masculine pitch is going to be very, very sexy coming out of that gorgeous woman's body of yours. Actresses train for years to get that low, husky quality.'

'I tell myself that too, on my good days,' said Gina

with a twisted smile. The trouble was that her good days were few and far between, especially trapped as she was at home with the melodious softness of her mother's and sisters' voices ringing daily in her ears.

Only later, when all the arrangements for her flight to Nandi and trip by charter supply boat to the island had been made, had Gina bothered to ask whose hospitality it was that she was availing herself of. By then it was too late to back down without getting involved in endless explanations. And how could she disillusion Daniel, who thought it was such a coup for a first novel to be published by Sterne Books? She was starting with the best, he had said. The senior editor he had shown her manuscript to, Kane Fletcher, was a friend of his, and quite willing for Daniel to act as her agent and editor on this one. As far as he was concerned everything was rosy.

To Gina it was bitter irony. There was a certain revenge here if she cared to take it. To have Leonard Sterne publish the book that told the story of her betrayal, it was almost funny.

She hadn't laughed when Daniel had mentioned that Sterne himself had a villa on Paradise. He had misunderstood her shocked reaction and hastily informed her that she needn't worry, she wouldn't get any visitors. Sterne rarely used the villa—'too far from the action if you get my drift'—and even when he did he valued his own privacy too much to invade anyone else's.

'You'll be quite on your own,' Daniel had soothed, 'and if you go stir-crazy or run into any artistic problems there's a radio-telephone at the villa. Call me.'

She hadn't called, loath to tell Daniel that so far his rest/work cure hadn't worked. And now she *couldn't* call. Not while Leonard Sterne was here. She was caught in a trap of her own making and there was nothing to do but sit it out.

CHAPTER TWO

In the warm, lazy light of a tropical morning Gina found her encounter with Leonard Sterne taking on a different perspective. She had acted foolishly and she was disgusted with herself, but it wasn't the end of the world. She had been tired after yet another unproductive day, and depressed, and it had been such a shock to meet him, even though she had had many dreams about meeting him again, about setting the record straight. But he hadn't been at all the contemptuous, brutal lion of a man she remembered. This Leonard Sterne had been teasing, tantalising ... He had physically restrained her, but he hadn't hurt her, and he had only deepened the kisses when he had sensed her involuntary response.

Gina stared at herself in the mirror as she brushed her long, black hair. No wonder he had mistaken her for a Fijian. Her olive skin had darkened to a deep tan and with her burnt almond eyes and thick, uncontrollably wavy hair she did look like a native. And the pareu she often wore because it was cool must have completed the picture.

She looked steadily into her own eyes, not letting her gaze drop below her chin. She had always felt like a changeling next to her mother and sisters. Diane and Eileen were the image of Margaret Bennett: blonde, blue-eyed and peaches-and-cream complexions. At fifteen Gina had desperately envied her elder sisters' nordic beauty and sophistication, she had wanted to be like them and had done her best to imitate their flip superficiality. The accident had changed that ambition forever, changed Gina, and now, at twenty-one, she was grateful for being 'different', being *herself* ... whatever that was, she told herself wryly.

She was setting up her drawing-board on the shaded verandah of the bungalow, where she liked to *try* and work before the sun became too hot, when she heard the plane. She put her hand up to her eyes and watched the red and white Lear jet circle the island before diminishing into the wild blue heavens. With it diminished much of her apprehension. She went into the compact kitchen to check her diary. She had taken off her watch as soon as she arrived, not wanting to know how much time she was idling away by swimming or sunbathing or merely avoiding facing the tasks she had come here to perform.

Of course, today was a Sunday! Leonard Sterne had probably only come for the weekend. Gina made herself a cup of coffee, topping it up with tinned milk before carrying it out to the verandah. She felt her spirits stir as she sat down on her stool and looked at the blank sheet of paper she had tacked on to her board. For the first time in months she actually felt like picking up her pencil.

To her surprise and delight she found the first few strokes easy. And then, suddenly, the ideas began to flow and the old, familiar excitement rose inside her. She *hadn't* lost her touch! She *could* still do it.

It was late afternoon before she broke off, her fingers stiff with cramp, and still the ideas crowded in on her. The story of the little boy's adventures on a remote, magical island ruled by an imperious magician was beautifully written but until now Gina had been unable to invest the main character with any vitality.

She stared now at the swirling figure of the magician that had come out of her pencil, wondering where he had sprung from. Usually her characters were built up slowly, by trial and error, but this one had definite ideas of his own. Yes, he was right . . . perfect . . . she would do the ink tomorrow and leave the colour washes until last.

She didn't actually see her visitor arrive but she felt a presence and turned quickly, her heart in her mouth.

The boy from last night was standing by the steps. Smaller and even thinner in daylight, his ribs showing clearly under his skin, he wore the same shorts and sneakers, but this time he carried a small basket made of woven palm leaves. Noting his mid-brown hair and the fine, straight features, Gina guessed that one of his parents, or perhaps his grandparents, must have been European.

She dipped her chin and smiled at him, putting off the moment when she would have to speak. He seemed wary, totally unlike the other shy but cheerful island children she had seen.

'Hello,' she croaked. Her voice sounded even more like a frog's than ever and she felt guilty for purposely forgetting to do the hated exercises this morning. The specialist's words rang in her ears,

'You'll never sound the way you used to, never have a perfect voice, but with therapy you'll smooth out a lot of the rough edges. For the first few months that you begin to use your voice I want you to keep speech to a minimum, and whisper rather than use full volume. Don't be dismayed if you find yourself "jamming" sometimes, it's quite natural, and in fact you might find that it always happens in times of extreme physical or emotional stress. Don't panic about it, just breathe deeply and wait until you're calm.'

'Have you come to visit me? Do you want your shells back, or are you just passing?' Gina asked the boy softly.

He frowned. Was his English poor?

'Would you like to come up and see what I've been doing?' she asked, holding out her hand to him.

He mounted the bottom step and then stopped, looking scared at his own temerity.

Gina reached behind her and unpinned the paper from the drawing-board. There was one way, at least, that she could always communicate with children. It was at a special pre-school centre for deaf children that she had first discovered her ability to transfer thoughts and feelings into pictures that delighted inquiring young minds. In a way that discovery had saved her sanity.

'See.' She held up her magician, a fiercely magnificent figure in flaring robes, an arm upflung to deliver a terrible spell.

The boy was transfixed where he stood, mesmerised by the picture, his brown eyes almost starting from his head. To her astonishment Gina saw him start to tremble.

'It's only a drawing.' God, for a soft and reassuring voice instead of this harsh grinding! 'If you like I'll——'

But he had dropped his basket and fled with a sound somewhere between a sob and a cry. Gina stared after him in dismay. She frowned at the drawing, hoping that his wasn't going to be the typical response. She wanted to excite the imagination, not terrify it.

She met the magician's eye and became transfixed herself.

'Oh, *no*!'

She took him apart, feature by feature, and put him back together again. No wonder he had come so easily! It hadn't been her imagination at work, it had been her memory. Her magnificent magician was Leonard Sterne! Was that why the boy had run off, because he recognised his parents' employer? Gina knew herself that Sterne could be pretty frightening at times and he would probably have little patience with children.

She slammed the picture back on to the board and tried a few subtle alterations. He was far too handsome for a wild magician anyway. She sharpened the jut of the jaw, but that only increased the likeness so she masked it with a dark pointed beard and winged the straight, even eyebrows, but when it came to the eyes she couldn't bring herself to put pencil to paper. Much as it galled to admit it the eyes were perfect ...

penetrating, compelling. In real life they were tawny coloured, like his mane of hair, speaking eyes that could burn like yellow flame and sear everything they touched on. In black and white they didn't have the vibrancy of the real version but they had a kind of fascination that matched the original. Even though they had only been glints in the darkness last night, there had been something about his eyes. They had certainly cast their spell over *her*. Gina touched her throat to remind herself, to arm herself. She hadn't been wearing her cameo up until now, there had been no need with nobody to see, no mother to urge her to cover up the scars!

'People don't know where to look, darling, it embarrasses them, and they are rather ugly.'

As if Gina didn't already know, as if she wasn't already self-conscious enough. Even in the darkness Leonard Sterne had recoiled from her scars. If he had been able to see them no doubt he would never have made the pass in the first place. Even Niven had ... Gina forced her thoughts back from the dangerous edge of the chasm.

Her eyes fell on the basket that her small visitor had dropped. She picked it up and investigated the clinking inside. There were a dozen or so shells, perfect specimens, shapes and colours which made Gina itch to sketch them. Had he been collecting them for himself, or had he seen her on the beach with her sketching pad, looking for odds and ends to build into the backgrounds of her illustrations? She put the basket in the kitchen. Perhaps he would come back for them. She hoped that he would, for there was a wistful quality about him that called to her, that made her want to make him smile, hear him laugh.

It was two days before she saw him again, and this time she didn't make the mistake of focusing her attention on her small visitor. She merely bent her head over her work, carefully inking in a line, pretending she didn't notice the scuffing sound that signalled his arrival beside the verandah.

He stood by the steps for a long while, then began edging up, crabwise. Gina still didn't turn, hiding her smile as she traced a curve with her pen. There was a cough, a shuffle and finally a stamping behind her on the verandah. She looked over her shoulder.

'Oh, hello.' She gave him a casual smile and returned to her drawing. He came so close that she could feel the prickle along the back of her neck, smell the salty sea-smell of him. From the corner of her eye she noted that his shorts were wet and there was a rim of fine sand clinging to his knees.

Carefully, making no sudden movements, Gina reached down to the folio at her feet and lifted out the sketch she had made the previous morning: a boy, crouched, intent on inspecting a beautiful shell. She studied it, head on one side, then risked an open glance at the boy's face. There was a brief flash of delight in the dark eyes as he recognised himself, quickly subdued, followed up by a stubborn, blank stare that Gina found disturbing. Why would he want to conceal his pleasure?

She moved her lips but nothing came out and she grimaced, realising that she had thrown herself so completely into her work that she hadn't done any exercises for days. She gestured her lack of voice to the boy, using some of the expression she had learned on a mime course she had taken as a desperate, constructive distraction during those five long months after the operation when she hadn't been allowed to try her voice at all.

The boy's reaction was as fierce as it was unexpected. He lashed out with a grunting cry, tearing the sketch of himself to pieces and scattering them over the bare boards of the verandah. His face was red under the dark skin, eyes screwed up into furious slits. In bewilderment Gina gaped at him and then as he turned to run away she caught him by the arm, so thin and bony that if felt as if it might snap at the slightest pressure.

He started to fight like a cornered animal and Gina fell to her knees to catch his hands. One evaded her grip and struck out, catching the ribbon that held the cameo around her throat, dragging it down to reveal the mass of scars. The boy froze in mid-blow as he saw them.

Gina let him go, bracing herself while she let him look. He seemed fascinated, tentatively reaching out to touch the worst of the scars. Gina flinched instinctively, as the memory of a bolder, more masculine hand intruded. The boy snatched his hand back.

'Hurt?' He mumbled so badly that Gina barely understood, but she was better equipped than most to understand distorted speech.

'Not any more,' she whispered. 'At least, not much.'

It had happened just before her sixteenth birthday. Already she had begun to taste the heady delights of being female. She had just acquired her first boyfriend, a swaggering super-macho eighteen-year-old, the possessor of a gleaming monster of a motorcycle. She had been showing off in front of her giggling friends that winter's day when he had collected her for a spin. She had been so busy preening that she hadn't noticed the long, dangling end of her scarf flap against the back wheel. As he had accelerated away it had caught and Gina had been jerked off backwards with such force that her larynx had been shattered. It was a miracle that she hadn't been strangled, or choked to death on her own blood, she had been told afterwards. But being told that you would probably never speak again was no miracle, it was a sentence of living death to a young, gregarious teenager.

Gina had wanted to die, but they wouldn't let her. Recovery had been painful and slow, complicated by infection and a series of unsuccessful operations to try and repair the damage. Unable to communicate except by laborious note-writing, Gina retreated into herself and stubbornly refused to accept help. For half a year she languished in a nightmare of self-imposed isolation. At home she was able to use a small computer to communicate, but it wasn't portable and, after their initial sympathy, her mother and sisters had acted with a mixture of embarrassed pity and impatience, only half-heartedly learning finger-spelling and signing. Going out was unthinkable, the frequent parties her mother gave things to be avoided with dread.

It had taken a brutal encounter with a hospital social worker to shock Gina out of her apathy. He had dragged her along to a special school for deaf children. He had shown her four- and five-year-olds who were profoundly deaf and yet who struggled to make and understand sounds; he showed her children who were blind as well as deaf, yet who were tenacious in their attempts to reach out to a world they barely comprehended. Gina had been deeply shamed and after her initial recoil she had gone back among the children and begun to learn what she *could* do rather than what she couldn't—like draw. She began to accept the fact that the world wasn't going to make any concessions just because she was now handicapped. It had been a long, hard, lonely road back, but she had made it ... and developed a protective shell along the way that the encounter with Niven had smashed with frightening ease.

'You talk!' The harsh accusation shattered her thoughts. She realised that she had automatically signed as she told him she had been in an accident, and the little face had hardened with bitterness.

A little, she mimed, then had an idea. Using the mirror attached to her drawing-board she showed him her exercises, first the muscular toning, followed by the breathing exercises and finally the phonetics. When she had completed the first sequence she turned to the silent watcher and pulled an expressive face. *You see?*

To her delight a slow smile crept into his eyes and spread downwards to tilt the corners of his mouth very slightly. She parodied her weariness and started in again, doing the full twenty minutes, conscious of the familiar flare of relief as her throat loosened up and the sounds began to come more easily.

He got bored after a while, but he didn't desert her. He began to leaf through the pile of papers on the little table next to the drawing-board. When Gina finally pushed the mirror away she found him frowning darkly at another sketch of the magician. She held her breath, hardly daring to move, afraid that he would tear it to pieces the way he had the drawing of himself. His lips were moving silently.

'Don't you like it? What's wrong with it?' Gina asked in her husky whisper. He ignored her for a long moment. Then he said:

'Bad. Bad.' In a thin, flat voice, devoid of emotion.

'No, he's not bad,' Gina shook her head positively. What was he . . . five or six? . . . his English didn't seem to be very good at all. How could she get the story across?

She beckoned him over to the drawing-board and quickly began to sketch a series of pictures depicting the story which was accompanying her illustrations. The magician was eccentric, autocratic, bad-tempered on occasion, but not evil. He created a magical world for the castaway boy and the ending, with the rescue of the boy by a passing ship, left leeway for more stories. Daniel was hoping that it would be the start of a popular series.

And idea which had been growing on her resolved itself as she finished the story with a flair. 'Will you be the boy?' she asked, pointing to the sketchy figure of the child. 'I need someone to model for me. Can I draw you?'

He stared at her suspiciously, confirming her theory even further. He was exactly right for the character of

Jao. There was something waiflike about his thinness, something fey about his wary countenance.

'I would pay you, of course. Money. I wouldn't expect you to do it for nothing.' She had a momentary qualm that she might be corrupting a young islander's innocence, like the colonial invaders of yore, but she consoled herself with the thought that if his parents did work at the villa, then they probably led a more sophisticated life than the inhabitants of the fishing village. 'Would you be able to? Do you go to school? Could you come afterwards perhaps?'

Slowly he pointed to the boy, then to himself, and to his open palm. He nodded gravely.

Gina held out her hand. 'Shake?' And when he didn't react, 'Shake hands, on the deal?'

His hand inched out and Gina shook it briefly and smiled, pointing to herself. 'Gina.' She repeated it several times, then wrote it out and showed him. 'Gina.'

He refused to say it but gave her his in exchange.

'Nick.'

'Nick?' Unsure she had it right. She passed him the pencil but he ignored it and scowled at her.

'Nick.' Slowly, grimly, he finger-spelled it out for her. N.I.C.

He glared at her, daring her so show shock. Gina fought to keep her expression under control as so many things about him were explained.

Nic was deaf, or at the very least suffered from greatly impaired hearing. It wasn't because he understood hardly any English that he spoke so rarely and with such difficulty. It also explained some of his wariness and unpredictability. He must have at first thought that she was mocking him when she tried to communicate in mime. How well she understood the frustration that must have engendered.

She stared at the boy, a mass of conflicting feelings welling up inside her. How ironic that she had come all this way to escape her problem only to find a reflection of it waiting for her. Her heart ached for the boy, for the questing intelligence she sensed was locked up inside him, but she didn't want to get involved. She had enough worries of her own without taking on the burdens of a little boy whom, after her month was up, she would never seen again.

It wasn't that she didn't know how to treat him, her contact with deaf children at the speech clinic and the pre-school centre had taught her much—a lot of it about herself and her own capabilities. It had been almost the only thing about Gina that her mother had approved of. Not only did her assistance at the centre keep her out of the way, it was also an acceptable part-time occupation for a Bennett. 'Charity work' her mother had called it, with a condescension that made Gina cringe.

The fleeting urge to withdraw her deal was conquered as Gina felt the fixity of his intense brown gaze. She could feel the tautness in him as he awaited rejection, and knew she couldn't do it.

'Will you be able to understand ... to know what I want you to do?' asked Gina slowly, signing as she went, feeling for the extent of his vocabulary.

He nodded, his little body seeming to expand as he realised that her attitude towards him hadn't changed.

'How old are you?'

He held up seven fingers and Gina hid her surprise. He was very small for his age. Had he been ill?

'Do you go to school?'

He turned his back, using the most potent form of resistance he knew and Gina shrugged.

'Let me show you what I want you to do.' She touched his shoulder and moved in front of him to speak. Carefully she explained how she wanted him to pose, and gave him some pencils and paper and three or four of her previous books to look at in case he got bored. As a general rule deaf children had more limited attention span than hearing children.

But Nic surprised her once more, with his ability to sit still for long stretches. Surprised her and worried her a little. It wasn't natural for any child to be so reticent, almost adult in his guarded responses.

As the days passed and they got used to each other Nic began to emerge from his shyness and assert an obstinate personality. As Gina plunged deeper into her work he became less wary, less willing to let her concentrate on anything other than himself. To get her attention he would sign questions, and when that didn't succeed, to indulge in tantrums. At first Gina coaxed him out of them, but when it got to the point that he was being destructive of her precious art materials she put her foot down and ignored his screams, going inside and shutting the door on him, hating herself for what she was doing to him, but knowing it was necessary if they were to respect each other.

Sometimes he didn't come back for a day or two after one of their tussles but usually, if his manipulations didn't work, he accepted it with a shrug that told Gina much. Such tactics obviously worked at home and he had become accustomed to overdramatising everything to get his own way.

In spite of her careful probing, Nic never talked about his family, or what he did when he was not with her. However she guessed that he had some kind of education, for he only turned up in the mornings, and his signing and finger-spelling were such that he must have had the benefit of a good teacher at some stage in his young life. He spoke but rarely and Gina refused to speculate on the reason. It was none of her business.

While the days passed swiftly, the evenings were profitless. Time and time again she picked up *The Long Silence* only to put it down again in frustration. Everything she tried to write was leaden and stale. The book oppressed her and she resented Daniel for forcing it back on her when she wanted so much to abandon it. She became more and more certain that she would never finish it and the knowledge of her failure nibbled away at her confidence.

Perhaps Nic sensed a new distraction in her for suddenly, one morning, he began to act up again and the old, wary, sullen cunning was back in his eyes. For three sessions in a row he did everything he could to provoke Gina, watching her with blank eyes that were a provocation in themselves. They were faintly accusing as if he was already anticipating her angry rejection and that made her feel even more defensive. Why was he doing it? To test her understanding? Or did he want her to lose her temper, to reassure himself that he still had the power to control situations the way he wanted to?

The morning that he spilled ink on two of her completed drawings was the last straw. But instead of turning on the defiant boy, Gina fled down to the beach and crouched on the sand at the water's edge, trembling with anger, afraid of the white-hot rage inside.

She didn't need this extra pressure. How had she forgotten how unpredictable deaf children could be— one moment co-operative and adorably affectionate, the next a seething ball of violent and self-willed emotion? She had thought that she and Nic had established a rapport, a tentative trust based on their shared difficulties. But it was never that simple. She felt, unfairly, that she had been manipulated into caring for Nic against her will. And now she was stuck with the consequences.

Absently, as a kind of soothing therapy, Gina began to build a castle in the sand. A shadow fell over the misshapen mound and she looked up, taken aback to see Nic. She had expected that he would have left to go and sulk by himself. His brown eyes were filled with an active dislike and Gina reflected her own mood. She wasn't ready, yet, to forgive him.

She read the intention in his face before he even moved and quickly smashed the castle down before he could do it for her. Amazingly the little act of childish spite made her feel marginally better. She crawled a few metres down the beach and started to build another.

Three ruined castles later Nic was joining in, building furiously and smashing his efforts with glee. They were both panting when they reached the end of the beach, by the rocky point, and looked back at the forlorn string of embattled ruins.

Suddenly they were smiling at each other, then giggling, then laughing uproariously as they rolled on the sand.

'Oh, Nic!' Gina's heart twisted at the innocent joy on his face. Whatever problems he had, Nic had a lot going for him. She hugged him tightly and for once he didn't wriggle at human contact.

'Oh, Gina,' he copied, in his flat little voice. It had taken him a while to get her name right but now every time he said it Gina felt a small jolt of warmth.

'We're a terrible pair,' she shook her head at him in mock despair. 'I'm sorry I've been a bit short with you lately, but my writing is not going well at all. I shouldn't take it out on my friends.' She tried to sign and hold on to him at the same time. It wasn't a success and they both toppled over and began to laugh again.

'I'm sorry, too,' said Nic awkwardly, able to say it now that Gina had shown the way. 'I get mad in here,' he pointed to his chest, 'and it hurts. It gets stuck.'

'I know, I know,' Gina ruffled his hair affectionately. 'It happens to me, too, sometimes.' She was pierced by surprise and delight as he leaned forward and quickly kissed her on the cheek, burying his hot face in the curve of her neck. It was the first spontaneous gesture of touching that he had made.

'What in the hell do you think you're doing? Let him go!' The harsh command shattered the fragile moment. Gina's eyes flashed open as she felt Nic's thin body wrenched out of her arms.

Leonard Sterne towered over her, bristling with hostility.

'What were you——' He stopped in mid-snarl as recognition ripped through him. *'You!'* The word was a single shot that echoed with shock and disgust in Gina's ears. The hostility strengthened to become open rage.

'I don't know what the hell you think you're up to, *Miss Bennett*, but you keep your grubby hands off my son!'

His son? Gina stumbled to her feet and stared from one to the other in bewilderment, suddenly seeing the similarities ... the skull structure, the lean build and easily tanned skin that she had mistaken for natural colouring in the boy. And the eyes ... different in colour but similar in shape. Oh God, the little boy who had so cunningly insinuated himself into her life was Leonard Sterne's *son*!

'Dominic!' A rigid hand tilted the boy's reluctant face upwards. 'Go back to the villa. Now! Miss Hamilton has been waiting for you to start your lessons.' Nic shrank from the repressed anger on his father's face, which only annoyed him further. 'And next time I see you I want you to be wearing that hearing aid, understand?' He signed as he spoke, quite efficiently, but Gina was too stunned to notice.

Nic scuttled silently away and Gina fought the urge to do the same as the voice lashed out,

'Not you. *You* stay!'

Gina lifted her chin proudly. He was a good six inches taller than her five foot eight and she resented it, conscious that to him she must look like a shabby urchin in her shrunken T-shirt and cotton shorts. But there was no evading him now that he had recognised her. It was time to stand up for herself, to reject the label he had stuck on her. He had thought the worst of her because that's what Niven had intended him to think but surely, eight months after that hideously embarrassing encounter, he would be willing to listen to the truth?

So she held herself proudly as his eyes moved with

contempt over her body. In white yachting trousers and a short-sleeved white shirt he looked cool and expensively casual, but there was nothing cool about his face. There was dark red colour under the tanned skin, the muscles stiff with angry distaste. The honey-coloured mane was longer than she remembered and a few silver threads glittered among the blaze of gold. The roughened stubble on his chin suggested that he'd come out without shaving and for a moment her focus slipped as she felt the fine-grained sandpaper of his cheek against her damp skin, the hot silk of his nakedness against her. To her horror she felt as if she was seeing right through his clothes to the fluidly muscular body beneath. Her long dark lashes flickered as she met the yellow fire of his gaze, terrified that he could read the lustful thoughts that she had consciously repressed since that night on the beach.

'Well, Miss Bennett?' he spat out. 'What in the hell are you doing on my island? Who brought you here?'

'I'm staying at the bungalow,' her rusty voice creaked, sounding feeble after his deep-throated snarl.

He swore and Gina's defensiveness faltered at the sight of the muscles bunching under the cotton-knit shirt as his body tautened. He was not only physically stronger than her, he also had a temper, and every reason, so he thought, to treat her with the utmost contempt.

'You're staying here with the writer ... Borelli, is it? *He* brought you here? He's supposed to be writing, not expending his energies keeping the likes of you satisfied.'

'I——' Gina hesitated. At least he hadn't so far connected her with the wanton native girl of a fortnight ago. With an effort she stopped herself touching the ribbon around her neck, to make sure it was hiding her disfigurement. Should she tell him now that she was Borelli? Now, while he was in a raging fury? What if he asked for proof? What if he wanted to see that agonisingly revealing manuscript? The thought made her go cold. He was reputed to be a man of extremely critical tastes, a perfectionist who demanded and expected to get only the best from the authors on his publishing list. Would he laugh at her pathetic effort? God, how could she bear to expose herself to him so completely?

The golden eyes narrowed to slits as her face, with its slanted cheekbones and disproportionately wide mouth, registered her indecision.

'Or perhaps he isn't keeping you satisfied. Is that why you're roaming around alone? Hunting for fresh meat? There'll only be lean pickings for you here.'

'I have plenty to keep me satisfied,' Gina began, intending to tell him about her illustrating. At least she could be proud of *that*.

'Then make sure you keep it that way!' he snarled at her. 'Because if I see you even *talking* to Dominic again I'll come down and kick you and your lover off this island, *personally*.'

'Nic's lonely——' Gina was determined not to let him have everything his own way. Didn't he care about his son's happiness?

'Don't you try and tell me about my own son!' His thunderous growl cut across her explanation. 'What in hell would a selfish bitch like you care about other people's feelings? You didn't care about my sister's, when you slept with her husband in her own bed! God knows why Borelli dragged you so far out of your native sewer, unless it was to get you away from another lover? Or was his wife beginning to catch on?'

'How dare you!' Gina gasped, breathless with rage, and the unfairness of it all. Here she was, at last with a voice to defend herself, and all she could do was stutter and stumble over feeble clichés while his insults flowed over her and stuck to her skin like burning black tar.

'I dare anything where Dominic is concerned, as

you'll find out it you don't lay off,' he said through his teeth.

'Then why is *he* roaming around alone?' Gina accused hoarsely, trying in her turn to wound. 'He should have friends, proper supervision. He's obviously not getting what he needs at home. He's dumped here like an unwanted package while you come and go as you please, how do you expect him to feel? What kind of father——' She broke off as the golden head was thrown back majestically, aware that she was trespassing in forbidden territory. She hardly knew anything about Nic, or his relationship with his father, but it was obvious that *something* was wrong between them.

'How I choose to bring up my son is none of your damned business!' He put her harshly in her place, his eyes burning with a feral intensity. An expression of loathsome speculation flickered across his face. 'What are you trying to do, get to *me* through Dominic?' He laughed harshly, in a way that made Gina flame with humiliation, despite her innocence. 'Sorry, *Virginia*,' his sneer mocked the inappropriateness of her name, 'but I know too much about you to succumb to that phony throatiness and pretended concern. I've seen you stripped for action, remember, and though your body might pass muster on a dark night I daresay it looks a little careworn at close quarters. Spoiled, promiscuous little rich-bitches like you tend to pall very quickly. Even Niven found that, didn't he?'

Gina went white at his monstrous arrogance. Although none of it was true, what he said filled her with shame.

'You know nothing about me. You're just making wild assumptions——'

'I didn't *assume* that you were in my brother-in-law's-bed, I *saw* you. Saw the total lack of shame that you flaunted in my sister's face. And not a word did you utter when Niven treated you like a cheap one-night stand. So it's quite natural, wouldn't you say, for me to assume that you're used to being treated like that? Perhaps you even enjoy it. With your upbringing I wouldn't be in the least surprised.'

Gina flinched, and he drove home his advantage. 'You see, I do know something about you. I once had the dubious pleasure of meeting your mother and sisters ... I was given the distinct impression that if I cared to exert myself I could score a hat-trick. *They* didn't appeal to me any more than you do.'

Gina thought she might faint. No wonder he was so virulent. She could just imagine the situation, the three blondes competing for his reluctant attention, unable to see his contempt for their own silly, selfish desires. She had tried to wall herself off from the embarrassment she felt when she saw or heard of another of her family's excesses but this struck deeply at her pride. The awful truth was that, but for that accident, Gina would have been like them—careless and uncaring—all the names that Leonard Sterne had called her. But she wasn't like that, she wasn't!

'Personally, I don't give a damn what sort of degradation you've chosen for yourself, but I will not have my son tainted by your sordid little mind. Understand? Stay away from him, Virginia, or I swear I'll teach you a lesson in humiliation that you'll remember every day of your idle, useless life!'

CHAPTER THREE

LEO jogged all the way back to the villa, running off his anger and the infuriating feeling of guilt. Damnit, why did she have to look at him with those great, dark, almond-shaped eyes as if he had inflicted a mortal wound? It wasn't as if she was a defenceless innocent, her sort toughened early and learnt all the tricks in the sex war. So why did he feel as if he had attacked a child? She had looked at him the way Dominic did, on the rare occasions that he risked an open stare ... all pain and silent accusation.

Dominic. In the two days since Leo had arrived on the yacht from Suva he had barely seen the boy. The temporary nanny obviously had little control over him, but was too scared—or too greedy—to admit it. Leo had been furious to find out that Dom had been in the habit of slipping out of the house in the mornings, even if his door was locked, and staying away for long periods. He had turned up for afternoon lessons with Miss Hamilton, who hadn't been aware of what was going on. She had reported, however, that Dom's work was still erratic and of poor standard. In some subjects he seemed to be going backwards and he still refused to speak more than the absolute minimum required to make his needs known. This morning Leo had decided that it was time to assert his parental authority, but he had been thwarted by Dom's early escape from the villa. It hadn't done his temper any good spending a fruitless hour and a half searching.

And then to find him as he had! Leo had almost exploded with savage resentment. Dom avoided strangers as assiduously as he avoided his father, so to find him laughing and playing with a strange woman

44

had been a shock. Standing on the rocks watching them, Leo had been shaken by a bitter, possessive jealousy that sent him plunging down to rip the happy pair apart. Dominic was his, yet he never laughed like that with Leo, or voluntarily touched him.

Leo had tried to keep his rampant emotion under control, knowing that the worst thing he could do would be to act harshly. But when he had recognised the girl his anger had shattered his control, and he had barked out orders like a drill-sergeant. Knowing the damage he was doing only spurred him on when he had turned on Virginia Bennett.

But, damnit, *how*? How in the name of sin had she managed to penetrate Dom's reserve? A woman like that?

Leo slowed down to a fast walk. He had felt like beating the living daylights out of her back there, simply for existing—for being there for Dom, for stealing some of the affection that was Leo's by *right*. He loved his son, in fact was surprised and somewhat disconcerted at the strength of his belated paternal feelings. He fiercely wanted to make up for the past few years, to form an open and loving relationship with the boy, but none of the moves he was making seemed to work.

But his over-reaction down there on the beach had been more than just an expression of parental wrath. He had almost bitten off his tongue when that accusation about her trying to get to him through Dominic had slipped out. He had been sure that a woman of her experience would leap on the arrogant comment as evidence of a transference of his own subconscious interest. Thank God she had been too mad to make the connection, to guess that he still carried an incredibly vivid picture of her lying semi-naked on a bed, hair black as ink tumbling across her bare shoulders. After the first shock of being interrupted by her lover's wife and brother-in-law she had been angry, rather than embarrassed. She had got off the bed and stalked across the room like a gypsy princess proclaiming her brazen dignity.

Even in the unflatteringly sordid circumstances, Leo had been shafted by envy of the man sharing the bed with her. Her body had been ripely sensual under the flimsy lace that enhanced rather than hid her charms, and the master stroke had been that black satin ribbon she had worn around her throat. It seemed to be a trade mark of hers, for today he had noticed that she was wearing a similar ribbon, with her shorts and T-shirt. Enough to give any man an erotic fixation.

But his initial envy of Niven had quickly waned. Virginia Bennett might not have the classical beauty of her mother and sisters, but that wild untameable darkness obviously drew its own share of attention and no doubt she had been trained since birth to take advantage of it.

Leo's face hardened as he recalled his one and only encounter with the rest of the Bennett family, a couple of months before the incident with Niven. It was the reason he hadn't even bothered to check on his brother-in-law's latest paramour ... he had known exactly what he would find. Margaret Bennett had gone all out to attract him, despite his obvious lack of interest, and when it at last sank in that she was going to get nowhere had gaily introduced him to her man-hungry daughters. With that sort of example to follow it was no wonder that the youngest in the family had gone off the rails.

Niven must have dropped her even before his divorce was through, because six months later he was married again, to a well-heeled widow, while Kathy was still desperately coping with her sense of failure. But that was the way of the world ... the innocent suffered while the self-centred, the shallow, forged ahead untouched by any honest emotion, like regret or remorse.

*　　*　　*

Gina didn't know how she got back to the bungalow. Her legs must have functioned independently from the rest of her. Once there she occupied herself with making a cup of hot, sweet tea, and sat down to sip it slowly until she felt her blood-sugar level rise sufficiently to stop her shaking.

Dominic Sterne. It wasn't surprising that she hadn't guessed, since Nic had shied away from any disclosure of his background. If Leonard Sterne had ever been married he certainly wasn't now ... not from what Daniel had told her. He had said that Sterne had a house in Auckland and a condominium in New York, and travelled a great deal, that's why he spent so little time in Paradise. He had also mentioned, in passing, that Sterne's name had been linked to women on both sides of the Pacific, usually writers or artists ... 'likes the independent type, the dedicated career woman who's not going to whine for attention,' Daniel had winked lecherously at Gina, 'except where it counts ... in bed.'

Gina hadn't risen to the bait. She couldn't care less, as long as he stayed off the island while *she* was there. But he hadn't, damn him! What was he doing back here? And why did Nic seem so frightened of him? In spite of her dislike of the man she found it hard to believe that Leonard Sterne would bully his son ... or any child. It was the weak, the powerless, the inept who usually struck out, and he was none of those things. He was the most alpha male Gina had ever come across.

She sipped her tea, which was as unpalatable as her thoughts. She had to face it, the reason that he had so effectively trounced her was that she was too aware of him. When he had sneered his incredible accusation that she had been trying to attract him she had almost let fly and smacked his arrogant face, but then he might have gone a step further, and proved his point, She *did* find him attractive, and that frightened her. It sapped her confidence and made her feel insignificant, untried

and unready. Was she a latent masochist, seeking
punishment to satisfy some obscure defect in her
character? Falling in love with Niven had been bad
enough, but this animal attraction she felt for Leonard
Sterne must be denied at all costs. She was glad now
that she hadn't told him the truth about that night he
had found her with Niven. If he despised her he would
give her a wide berth. Let him lump all the Bennetts
together, it was her best protection. The empty,
hedonistic lifestyle of her sisters, and their unsavoury
reputation in certain quarters of their social circle, was
suddenly an advantage, where it had once been a
burden. It was a shame about Nic, but their friendship
would never have come to anything anyway. Perhaps,
though, she could send him a copy of *Jao and the
Magician*, once it was published.

She worked hard over the next few days, half-
expecting to be ordered off the island at any moment.
But Leonard Sterne seemed to have contented himself
with threats and she was left in peace. It surprised her
how much she missed Nic and a small part of her hoped
that he, too, was missing her a little. As the illustrations
neared completion, her other problem crowded out her
regrets: soon she would have no excuse not to sit down
at the typewriter and wrestle with *The Long Silence*.

One evening, as she went for her final swim of the
day, she became aware of an almost palpable feeling of
unease. There was a yellowish cast to the sky and the
air was quite still. The quietness was complete, too: no
seabirds wheeled above the outer stretches of reef crying
their presence in the salt-laden air.

Not knowing whether her imagination was playing
tricks on her, Gina went in to prepare a simple salad for
dinner, but found it too hot and oppressive to eat
much.

She went to bed early, switching on the bedside lamp
as the sun fell into the sea, unable to help noticing that
the usual profusion of moths and insects didn't start

beating at the insect screens that covered the slatted windows.

Her sleep was restless and invaded by nebulous dreams and when the knocking came, at first it seemed part of her dream. When she realised that she was awake, and somebody was knocking at her door, Gina felt her mouth go dry. Who else would it be but Leon Sterne, come to throw her off the island? Disoriented by sleep it didn't strike her as odd that he should make his move in the dead of night. Hurriedly she pulled on her jeans and a cotton top, needing the confidence of clothes, and stumbled out to the door. She flung it open defiantly and stared, open-mouthed, not at the king of the beasts but at the cub shivering on her doorstep.

'G . . . Gina?'

'Nic! What on earth——?' Her shock turned to concern as she saw his pinched face. 'Nic, are you all right? What's wrong?' She grasped his thin shoulders and bent to put her face on a level with his. 'Nic?'

'I'm scared!' The thin, high wail tore at her heart, and Gina was instantly protective. What was that wretched father of his thinking about, letting the boy out at night in only thin pyjama shorts? It was quickly followed by the realisation that probably he didn't know, and that was even more disturbing.

'You'd better come in.' She led him into the kitchen and pushed him gently into a cane chair beside the rather rickety wooden table. She knelt and took his small, cold hands into hers. 'Now, Nic. You must tell me what's happened.'

'S . . . storm.' He stuttered so badly she had difficulty understanding.

'Storm? There's no storm, Nic.' As she spoke she heard the rattle of leaves outside and wondered if she had spoken too soon.

'C . . . coming,' he whispered miserably, his eyes huge, swallowing up his little face.

'I see, there's a storm coming,' she repeated, so he

knew that she understood, using her hands too so that what he couldn't hear or lip-read, he could see. 'Are you afraid of storms, Nic?'

He drew his mouth in and nodded once, sharply.

'But why did you come here? Does your father know that storms frighten you?'

He flinched and looked away but Gina firmly turned his head back, and repeated the question. He gave a half-shake, half-nod that could have meant anything and Gina tried to mask the angry desire to push him further. If Leo Sterne didn't know then he damned well should! That Nic would brave the darkness to come here to her, rather than turn for comfort to anyone in his own household, confirmed the worst of Gina's suspicions. Gina put her arms around Nic and let him bury his head against her. She rocked him softly, talking gently to him. Even if he couldn't hear her words he could feel the comforting vibrations in her chest.

After a while she stroked back his hair and lifted his face again. 'Your father told you not to come here, didn't he?'

He nodded, tears shimmering in his eyes. It occurred to Gina that she had seen him furious, frustrated, happy and sad, but she had never seen him cry. Had someone told him little boys didn't cry? Leo Sterne perhaps? Right now tears might have helped ease the tension in his small body.

'You'll have to go back, Nic,' she said, going on quickly as she saw the panic rise. 'Don't worry, I'll come with you. Does anyone know that you're gone? Will they be looking for you?'

'Not go back.' His lower lip jutted.

'Why not, Nic, why don't you want to go back?' she probed. His eyes slid away from hers and back again, carefully shuttered.

I hate storms, he signed.

'I know. But you'll be safe inside the house.' *Safe in the house*, she reiterated in sign. He erupted with a suddenness that sent Gina staggering back, screaming at the top of his voice the barely coherent words,

'Won't go back. Afraid. Afraid! Lock me in. Can't get out. The storm! The storm!'

Gina watched the contortions of his face with rising horror. Surely he didn't mean that he was locked in his room, alone, at night? My God, what kind of household was it! The poor little boy was utterly terrified and almost hysterical at the thought of going back to his home. She had a good mind to keep him here, but in all conscience she couldn't. She could, however, give Leonard Sterne the tongue lashing he deserved. And he had the nerve to sneer at Gina! Breaking up a marriage was a pristine sin next to ignoring a terrified child.

'It's all right, Nic,' she soothed. 'I'll come with you. I'll make sure you're not frightened any more, don't worry.' Her own fears and problems paled against Nic's.

'Stay, please, stay! Please, Gina?'

Nothing that Gina could do or say seemed to calm him. He looked so pitifully small as he begged, so vulnerable, so . . . *unloved*, eventually her heart melted completely. Perhaps, if his door was locked, he wouldn't be missed until morning anyway. It was after ten now and possibly everyone else at the villa has also gone to bed early. Besides—she heard the rattle of rain against the side of the bungalow—knowing what these tropical downpours were like she and Nic would be drenched to the bone before they got fifty metres. Perhaps it would be best, after all, to keep him here with her and confront Leo Sterne in the morning.

All the while she thought these things she knew that they were only feeble justifications for her action. She *wanted* Nic to stay. She wanted to comfort him and soothe his fears . . . she understood what it was like to be prey to nameless black panic . . . and also, a corner of her admitted, she thought that Sterne deserved a good fright if he found his son was missing. Perhaps then he might make more of an effort to be a parent!

'All right, Nic, you can stay. But I must take you home first thing in the morning, OK? No fuss—first thing in the morning!'

A ghost of a smile curled his shaking mouth and he nodded. All that probably got through was her first words, Gina realised, but at least he no longer looked stricken.

Gina made some hot cocoa and they sat in the kitchen and drank it. She made Nic tell her how he had got out of the house, through his window, and how things had seemed to chase him in the darkness.

'It was probably only the wind. It was brave of you to even come out when you knew the storm was coming. How did you know about it?'

Her small flattery tricked him into answering truthfully. '*He* said it was on the radio,' he said, then scowled at her. Another gust of wind shook the house and he jumped and his hands clenched on Gina's arm.

Now she knew why she had been uneasy earlier. It had been the calm before the storm. She had a momentary qualm. Would they be safe here? The bungalow was on level ground and the tide was full tonight. What happened if the storm whipped up the lagoon? Unlike the villa, which was built further back, among the protection of a series of ridges, this place was fully exposed to the elements.

She hid her disquieting thoughts from Nic and distracted him with a few noisy games of snap before giving him another cup of cocoa, laced with a tablespoon of brandy. To her relief this seemed to make him drowsy, despite his fear, and she took him through to her bedroom and tucked him into her bed, after finding him one of her soft, well-washed T-shirts to wear. But as she turned to leave to make up the bed in the other room, Nic clutched at her frantically.

'No! Don't go. Stay, Gina, stay!'

Why not? If the storm did turn out to be fairly fierce, Nic might need reassurance through the night, anyway. Gina slipped her short, loose white cotton nightie back on and crawled in beside him. She felt a wave of deep affection for the little figure snuggling up to her. Nic fell asleep within minutes, snoring slightly, which made Gina wonder whether she might have given him a little too much brandy. Still, at least he seemed peaceful, his bony body warm and relaxed, and utterly trusting.

Gina hoped that the trust was justified as she listened to the storm build up outside. She wasn't too keen on them herself but she refused to let her fears conquer her common sense, and when the banging started she refused to entertain the possibility that the house was falling down around her ears. It was a shutter come loose and she would have to get up and fasten it or she would never get any sleep.

She got up reluctantly, glad that the earlier, sticky heat had given way to a moist cool, and padded out to track down the errant shutter. It was only when she went towards the front of the bungalow that she realised that it wasn't a shutter at all.

'Open up in there, damn you, or I'll break this door down!'

The roar sounded above the harsh rattle of the wind and Gina knew with a sinking feeling that her earlier premonition was realised. The door shivered violently on its hinges and she ran to unfasten it.

She was unprepared for the blast of wind that flattened her thin gown against her body and sent her two steps back into the room, far enough for Leo Sterne to pounce over the doorstep and force the door shut behind him.

He had a black oilskin coat on that dripped rivulets on to the coconut-grass matting. His mane was darkened by the rain and plastered to his head, his rain-slicked face as stormy as the weather.

'Where is he?'

Gina hugged herself defensively against the savage demand.

'I said where is he, Virginia?' he thundered. 'I know he came here—there's nowhere else for him to go!' He made to push past her towards the darkened bedrooms but Gina caught him by the arm and in turn had her arm grabbed violently. His oilskin brushed against her gown, dampening it so that it clung to her legs.

'I—he's asleep,' she said huskily, trying unsuccessfully to free her arm. For a moment she thought her vision was being affected by his presence, then she realised that it was actually steam rising from his shoulders. His hand felt hot on her bare skin and she guessed that the combination of intense physical exercise and the rain had produced the phenomenon. Wryly she conceded that Leo Sterne was steaming both physically *and* emotionally.

'Where? In there?' he hammered out, jerking his head in the direction of her room.

'Yes, but I don't think you should wake him. I——'

'*You* don't think!' Now that he had found his son he paused long enough to vent his temper. 'Lady, I warned you once before about poking your nose into my life. What kind of moron would encourage a boy to sneak out of his home in the middle of the night and——'

'Wait a minute!' Gina wrenched her arm out of his grasp and began to steam lightly herself. '*Encourage? Are you talking about me? I haven't seen Nic for days, let alone encouraged him to do anything.'* She forgot about her flimsy nightgown, her wildly tumbled hair, her eyes almost black with temper as she raised her voice hoarsely over the sound of the wind. It was a strain but she was too riled to bother about a little pain. 'If he did anything wrong it's because of *you*, not me.'

'I didn't come here to listen to a lecture on child psychology, I came here to get Dom,' he growled fiercely, the big cat's eyes flickering over her face as his body shifted threateningly.

'If you go in there in the mood you're in you'll frighten him all over again!' Gina accused furiously. 'Don't you *know* that's he's terrified of storms? He turned up here absolutely petrified. It took me ages to calm him down.'

His whole body bunched and for a moment Gina thought he was going to hit her. A pulse throbbed heavily in his temple and his jaw clenched visibly. 'I'm well aware of my son's fears, thank you, far more so than you,' he gritted, when he had got himself under control.

'Then why weren't you there with him when he needed you?' Gina demanded, refusing to back down. 'Why did he have to come all this way to a virtual stranger for comfort? How could you lock that poor, frightened little boy in his room when you knew that he——'

'Lock him in his room! What in the hell are you talking about!'

'I . . . he said . . .' Gina faltered in the face of his genuine startlement, straining to remember exactly what Nic *had* said.

'You obviously don't know my son as well as you claim you do,' he said, with twisted satisfaction at her uncertainty. 'He's very good at making up stories to get sympathy from gullible strangers.'

Gina flushed, knowing that she had swallowed Nic's story without question because it was just the sort of thing she could imagine the arrogant, insensitive Leo Sterne doing.

'For your information, he was *not* locked in his room, and I *was* with him until I had to go and check that——'

'You left him, all alone, in the state he was in?' cried Gina in outrage.

'No, dammit!' he yelled at her. 'I left him with his

tutor. He ran away from her. She's got a broken leg. By the time she got downstairs to tell me he was well gone.'

'I still think that whatever you had to do could have waited until——' Gina began stiffly, hating to appear in the wrong yet again, before this intimidating man.

'The hell you do!' he swore. 'You think I should have left the place open for the cyclone to sweep clean?'

'Cyclone?' Gina blanched. 'What cyclone?'

'What do you think this is?' A large raised hand indicated the noise outside. It was even worse than before but Gina had been too incensed to notice.

'I . . . Nic said a storm was coming, he didn't say a cyclone.'

'He doesn't know what one is.' His thick eyebrows rose sarcastically. 'No doubt I should have tried to terrify him some more by telling him about it. Didn't you hear the radio warning?'

'I haven't got a radio,' Gina said numbly, feeling the stirrings of fear herself. People got killed in cyclones.

'There's one in the storeroom; didn't you even look? Don't you know that it's an elementary safety precaution on isolated islands like this?' he said angrily. 'No, of course you don't. What you know could be fitted in the head of a pin . . . except with regard to sex. I'm sure that you could fill an encyclopedia with your knowledge on that subject!'

Gina fingered the ruffle at her throat nervously, automatically smoothing it up over her scars. Almost everything she owned had little stand-up collars or ruffles or roll-necks, even her night-wear. She wasn't sure why he had suddenly introduced sex into the argument but it had the effect of sending all her insecurities toppling down on her. She swallowed a slight roughness in her throat. She had been talking too much and too forcefully, and she would pay for it later. But for the moment she needed to defend herself against her rising awareness of the man opposite. She plucked her gown where it clung to her thighs and then regretted it when she saw the tawny eyes slide down to her hips, and below. Could he tell she wasn't wearing anything underneath? By clenching her hands she managed to stop herself trying to hide behind the age-old maidenly gesture of modesty. He looked up again, at her face, and she felt a tingle all the way down to her toes at what she read in his eyes. He knew. He could see; and he seemed amused by her nervous confusion.

She cleared her throat. 'About Nic ...' To her disgust her voice dropped deeply and his gaze sharpened as he heard what he thought was a huskily provocative murmur.

'I'll go and get him,' he said tersely.

'No, I'll do it, you might scare him,' she intervened.

'He is *my* son,' he hissed at her, and this time even Gina could hear and see the blow she had dealt him.

'I meant, he doesn't expect to see you here, he might be startled,' she found herself whispering gently.

'That's not what you meant at all.' His mouth was tight, the narrow upper lip a thin line, and the eyes as hard as gold nuggets. 'Why bother to spare me? You haven't so far. It's quite evident you see me as some kind of inhumane monster.'

'I ... I'll come with you to get him up,' she said, avoiding his frowning glare.

'You can get some of your things too. And wake Borelli.'

Gina stopped in her tracks and turned, putting out her hands as he almost ran into her in the narrow hall. His chest was broad and solid beneath her spread fingers and she snatched her hands back as if she had been burnt by the contact.

'What did you say?'

'You're coming back to the villa with us.'

Gina shook her head vehemently, the dark waves shimmering over her shoulders. 'I'm not the one who's afraid.'

'You're too stupid,' he insulted her succinctly. 'Do

you *know* what a cyclone is? What it's capable of? It's a hurricane. It could rip through this place as if the walls were made of tissue paper. The cyclone's on a direct path for Fiji so we might not get the full brunt of it, but it'll be bad enough.'

'You think the bungalow will be damaged?' asked Gina hoarsely.

'It's certainly not hurricane-proof. The villa is. It's reinforced concrete, set well back into the ridge. But we'd better move *now*, before this thing strikes.'

Gina shuddered. 'I suppose I have no choice.' She was half-inclined to say she'd rather brave a night with a hurricane, than cooped up in the same building with him, but she held her tongue.

'Not if you want to live, no,' he said impatiently. 'Now, can we get on with it? Only take what you and Borelli can carry because I'm not here to play valet. I'll carry Dom.'

'Er . . .'

'What is it this time!' he barked at her flushed face.

'There's no Borelli, at least there is, but there's not anyone else . . . just me and Dominic.'

'Are you drunk?' He leant closer and Gina shied nervously.

'Of course not!' she snapped. 'What I'm trying to tell you is that there is no such *man* as Borelli. I'm Borelli, it's my pen-name.'

He laughed sharply. 'Pull the other one, sweetheart. What happened? Did he get fed up with you and take the supply-boat home?'

'Look, I'm telling you the truth,' Gina put her hands on her hips, not realising that her gesture pulled the thin cloth taut over her full breasts. 'You can check up if you like. Kane Fletcher is the man who organised this trip for me to work on my book. I'm Borelli.'

'No kidding?' He didn't believe her, that much was obvious from his sardonic expression. 'You must be one sweet operator if you could talk your way around

Kane. Or maybe it wasn't all *talk*. What are you writing, a sex manual ... or maybe a kiss-and-tell exposé ... did you dazzle my hard-headed editor with a sample for review?'

Words failed her, so Gina settled for a burning glare. She tossed the heavy swathe of hair back and led him down the hall, hoping that he was going to be thoroughly humiliated when he found out that she was exactly who she said she was.

'In here.' She went over to the bed and turned on the lamp, bending down to pull back the covers so that Leo Sterne could lift his son. Nic moved feverishly but it was evident he was deeply asleep as Gina gently brushed the hair off his thin face, smiling faintly at the picture he made smothered in the folds of her T-shirt. She looked enquiringly at Leo Sterne when he made no move to pick the boy up and found him studying her with a strange expression on his face.

'I thought you said we didn't have much time,' she reminded him uneasily, and he scooped his son up as if Gina had accused him again of neglect. He looked down at the sleeping head possessively and frowned.

'He's still dead to the world. Did you drug him? He's usually a light sleeper.'

'I gave him a little brandy,' Gina admitted at the sword-point of his suspicion.

'Brandy! What are you trying to do, turn him into an alcoholic?'

'I doubt whether one tablespoon in a cup of cocoa is going to hurt him,' Gina snapped. 'He was frantic, I thought it best if I could make him relax a little.'

He growled something under his breath, nothing complimentary, Gina was sure, and paused to flick off a cover and wrap it around the small body. 'Are you coming?'

Gina scurried about, stumbling into some clothes and stuffing others into a small bag. She wouldn't put it past him not to wait for her. As she collected her precious portfolio of drawings and hovered beside the pile of manuscript she listened for the door above the growing noise of the storm. She was tempted to leave the wretched book to be shredded by the hurricane, but she couldn't do that now that she had confessed her identity to Leo Sterne. He would probably sue her for breach of contract, even if she hadn't actually signed anything yet. He would make her sign, *then* sue her!

She was struggling into a lightweight raincoat, which was the only kind she had, and juggling her load as she hurried back out into the lounge. The lion was twitching impatiently, having unbuttoned his voluminous oilskin and rebuttoned it over the sleeping figure in his arms.

'I've turned off the generator,' he explained tersely as she screwed up her eyes in the darkness. 'Come on, I'm not waiting any longer. And don't expect me to cope with any hysterics out there. You either make it under your own steam, or you don't make it at all.'

Hysterics! Gina ground her teeth as they stepped into the teeth of the wind. He sounded as if he *expected* her not to make it. If it wasn't for Dominic he would probably never have bothered to check up on Borelli and his 'mistress', and warn them about the cyclone. Well, Virginia Bennett was not going to be blown away by a hurricane for *anyone's* convenience, much less this insulting devil!

CHAPTER FOUR

TWICE on the trip to the villa Gina was blown over by the force of the wind. The second time she watched helplessly as her hand-grip tumbled away among the trees. Clutching her folio she called ahead to Leo Sterne to wait while she ran back, but the wind took away her words and he continued to stride ahead. Dominic had woken and begun to struggle, screaming, in his father's arms, and with one despairing look behind her Gina hurried forward to mouth reassurances through the black hair whipping in stinging lashes across her face.

She stumbled along in the wake of the tall, black-clad man, sand and rain flaying her exposed skin and scouring her eyes and mouth. The palm-trees were bowed under the howling gale and the grass and undergrowth boiled in green imitation of the furious sea.

Trying to conquer the panicky feeling that she was drowning on dry land, Gina managed to keep up until at last the villa came into sight. She shivered with cold and relief as they were admitted into a dim entranceway by a brawny young Fijian who barred the door behind them.

Leo Sterne put down his struggling burden and stripped off his oilskin, speaking tersely. 'If you've shuttered all the windows, Thomas, get Liana to put some warm clothes on Dominic and go and help Miss Hamilton. I want everyone in the dining-room, it's the safest part of the house.'

But Dominic backed away from the young man, saying shrilly, 'I want Gina, I want Gina!'

Flinging a single, contemptuous look at the bed-raggled woman clutching the zipped satchel to her chest as if it was a life-buoy, Leo Sterne laid down the law. 'First you get dry and dressed, Dom. *Then* you may see Miss Bennett.'

'Now! Now!' Nic ignored his father's signing but instinctively knew what he was saying. He flung himself towards Gina, only to be caught and held by powerful arms.

'No, Dom——'

'I want Gina! Gina!' He pinched and scratched at the restraining arms and Leo Sterne swore, turning his face away from his distraught son to snarl at Gina, 'What in the hell have you done? Hypnotised him?'

'You said you'd stay,' the boy sobbed, reaching out with such a pathetic gesture that Gina was shaken out of her frozen stillness.

'I ...' Helplessly she looked from father to son, quailing before the one and inextricably drawn towards the other.

'Tell him to go with Thomas,' Leo Sterne told her furiously. 'Obviously your word is law to him, *tell him!*'

'Nic, please ...' Gina's voice broke, raw and sore from the physical battering her throat had put up with tonight.

'For God's sake, can't you forget that phony throatiness of yours for once, at the moment it's about as appealing as a buzz-saw!' His disgust ripped into her, making her blanch at the cruelty.

Dominic had stopped fighting his father and was looking at them both with a frown. His father's face was tight and stiff, wearing the dark mask that Nic hated, and Gina was very pale, her eyes so sad that he felt something painful swell inside him. *He* was making her look like that. *He* was hurting her because she was Nic's friend. He would make her go away, like Mummy, like Fenny. Rage made him forget the promise he had made to himself never, never to talk to *him* ...

'You leave her alone. She's my *friend*.'

The two adults looked at him with identical expressions of shock at being addressed so clearly and grammatically and Dominic felt immense satisfaction, for the first time feeling the power of words over the power of silence.

'I don't want to live with *you*. I want to live with Gina.' The restraining hands fell away and Nic glared at his father. The mask slipped and the brief darkening of the golden eyes suddenly made him feel funny and squirmy inside. Nic hurried on, trying to make the horrid queasiness go away. 'I love Gina, I don't love *you*.'

Although the world vibrated around them with the sound of the storm outside the concrete walls it seemed to Gina as if there was a long, breathless hush, broken by Leo Sterne's bitter accusation.

'My God, you really have done a number on him.' His voice rose from a tight snarl to a full-throated roar. 'I should have gone with my first instincts and left you out there in that bloody hurricane. What have you been telling him? What lies have you been feeding him?' Her silence drove him to the brink of black madness. 'Say something, you dumb bitch! Answer me, damn you——' He reached for her, but his son was in between them, pushing, holding them apart, sobbing dry-eyed.

'Stop it! Just because she can't talk! Stop it! Leave her alone. Her voice is broken. She's like me——'

Leo Sterne went absolutely still, letting his son push him away as if the boy was the stronger of the two. The storm, Dominic, the astonished Thomas, all were forgotten as the man and woman faced each other, a current of pure, white-hot, unidentifiable emotion arcing between them.

'You heartless little slut!' he hissed savagely at her, yet with a flare of triumph that was at odds with his words. 'Is that how you got him to trust you—by playing a cruel trick on him . . . on a *child*?' He bent closer and said viciously, 'Speak to him, go on, show him how his *friend* lied to him. Go on, Virginia, or I swear I'll wring the words out of you!'

He grabbed the hand that was rubbing tensely at the upright collar of her drenched blouse and dragged it aside, bringing up another large hand to encircle her throat, forcing her chin up.

Gina tried to pull away: 'Don't——'

She knew the exact instant that he saw the thin vertical red line that ran out of the top of her collar almost to the point of her lower jawbone. His hand dropped as if he had been stung.

'My God ...!' It was scarcely a breath but the appalled expression on his face was so familiar that it made Gina curl up inside. She turned to Nic, not wanting to see the distaste, the pity, that usually followed on the realisation that she was disfigured.

'Nic, please, you really must get dry,' she grated hoarsely, not bothering to sign when she saw his frightened eyes fixed on her lips. 'I do too.' She plucked at her clothes. 'I'll be here when you come back, I promise.'

His lower lip trembled and he gave a quick, nervous, sideways look at his father who stood stiffly, hands clenched at his sides as he stared at Gina's downbent head. She summoned a shaky smile, guessing the boy's worried thoughts. 'I'll be all right.'

With one last, backward look, Nic trotted after Thomas. Gina straightened, wrapping her arms around her body, trying to drive off the chills that mingled with hated embarrassment. Now he was going to be sorry for her and she was thoroughly fed up with being pitied.

'It was true, then?' he said with a harsh incredulity, as if he still didn't believe the evidence of his eyes.

'I can talk,' she admitted stony-faced. 'But not very well yet.'

He turned abruptly. 'Come. I'll show you where you can get dry, and find something for you to wear.'

He strode off and Gina stared after him open-mouthed for a moment before she followed, fuming. He couldn't even apologise! He wasn't even curious, though she should be feeling relieved rather than annoyed that he wasn't plying her with questions. If anything he seemed even more angry than ever, as if it was a disappointment to discover that she wasn't a heartless slut after all. Pig!

The darkened corridor was lit by kerosene lamps hung from the heavy beams which supported white ceilings, their flickering flames dancing across the rough-cast walls to make them seem alive with little dancing devils. When he came to the third doorway in the wide hallway Leo Sterne stopped to unhook one of the lamps and carried it into a large square bedroom. He put the lamp down on a table by the bed.

'Our generator's off for safety reasons and it's too dangerous to take a bath in this weather so you'll just have to rub yourself down to get warm. There should be clothes more or less your size in that chest in the corner. I'll send Liana to get you—and make sure you bring the lamp with you, we don't want to risk a fire.'

Whose clothes? Gina felt like asking. Cast-offs from cast-off mistresses? But beggars can't be choosers and since she had lost her own . . . her thoughts came to an abrupt halt. Her folio! She must have dropped it when Sterne had grabbed her! She spun towards the door.

'Where in the hell are you going?'

She stopped at the cracking command. 'My f— my satchel, I left in in the hall.'

'Has it got clothes in it?'

'No, just papers,' she croaked, and he gave an angry exclamation as he moved past her.

'Papers aren't going to be any use to you now. Leave it. I want everyone together when this thing hits, so get moving!'

'Oh, but——' To her horror Gina was overtaken by a sneeze. Then another. She felt the pressure building up to a third and moaned, panic scattering reason. Not a cold! She couldn't have caught a cold in such a short space of time. Oh God, what if she had! What if the infection affected her throat, hindered the healing? She sneezed again and felt the pain under her jaw, found herself fighting for breath as she had out in the storm, wheezing like an asthmatic as she sucked in fearful breaths.

'Miss Bennett? Virginia?' Leo Sterne had been arrested by her moan, and the way that colour had suddenly drained from her face.

His sharpness barely pierced her disintegrating composure and she lifted both hands to press against her throat, to try and force away the tightness.

'Is it your throat? Are you in pain?' When she didn't answer he came back, the words dragged out of him with angry reluctance. 'Did I hurt you? Damnit, answer me!'

'No ... I ...' The words were a bare husk interrupted by a sneeze. 'I mustn't get a cold. The doctor said I mustn't get a cold.'

'Well, what are you standing around wasting time for?' he snapped impatiently. 'Oh, for God's sake——' He strode across the room and through another darkened doorway and came back holding a thick white bathsheet. He pushed it at her and she took it blindly, her hands shaking so much that she dropped it.

He swore and snatched it up again. 'Are you going to rub yourself down or shall I do it for you?'

He flung the towel over her shoulders and reached out to flick open the first two buttons of her blouse. 'I don't suppose it makes much difference to you if I see you naked, I've already seen you as near as damnit. And I suppose I must be one of the few men of your acquaintance who don't want to bed you.'

His hateful sarcasm succeeded in halting Gina's descent into hysteria. *You did the other night*, she felt like flinging in his face, but she restrained herself, knocking his hands away and snatching the towel against her gaping blouse.

'Get away from me, you pig!'

He smiled nastily and backed off with a shrug. He went over to the chest and opened it, producing a few items of clothing after a brief rummage. He flung them on the bed and strode to the door.

'No underwear there, I'm afraid, but from what I hear the Bennett girls don't like to slow themselves down by wearing any.'

Gina trembled with fury as she dried her matted hair and peeled off her clothes. Brute! And she had thought he would pity her! Beast!

As she took off her blouse she realised that he couldn't but have noticed that she wasn't wearing a bra. It was practically transparent with wetness and her nipples were tight with cold.

She dressed jerkily in the cotton trousers and buttoned the loose shirt to her neck, so intent on heaping insults on his absent head that it wasn't until she picked up the lamp that she realised she was breathing freely, and that her throat, although slightly sore, wasn't obstructed. Talking too much had caused the tightness, that's all.

As she went out into the hall she met a slim, pretty Fijian girl gliding towards her.

'Hello, I'm Liana,' she smiled, speaking above the wind. 'I'm Thomas's wife—in charge of the household. If you follow me I'll show you where everyone is.'

Gina followed her lithesome sway down the now-dark corridor. As they passed through the hallway where they had entered the house she looked in vain for her folio. If Leo Sterne had picked it up she only hoped that he had the decency not to pry.

The rooms they passed through were all square, all tiled in plain slate with white walls and ceilings and furnished with a luxurious simplicity that screamed money. Finally they reached a big room lit by two huge brass lamps. It was windowless, Gina guessed designed for just this eventuality, yet the light natural-wood

furniture stopped it feeling at all claustrophobic. There
were five people gathered around two curving couches
at the end of the room. One of them was Nic, who
immediately wriggled out of the grasp of a tall red-
headed woman and ran towards Gina.

I told you I'd be here, Gina mouthed at him and he
grinned his relief. He mightn't hear the storm, but he
must be able to feel the frightening vibrations and
although he was warmly dressed in overalls, the hand
that he slipped into hers was cold and tense.

Leon Sterne, who had been bending his head towards
Thomas, stepped forward as they approached. He had
changed too, into dark trousers and a white sweatshirt
with padded insets at the elbows and shoulders. Trust
him to look elegant, even in the midst of a hurricane.

'Miss Bennett.' His deep voice rumbled under the
storm. 'This is Pamela Smythe, Dominic's companion.
Virginia Bennett.'

The attractive redhead didn't smile, her eyes shifting
edgily with every sound from outside. She was in her
mid-twenties and obviously experienced with deaf
children, otherwise she wouldn't be here with Nic, yet
she was making no attempt to reassure or communicate
with the scared little boy. She seemed more concerned
with clutching on to her employer's sleeve.

'And this is Aileen Hamilton, Dom's tutor.'

The middle-aged woman on the couch leaned
forward to shake Gina's hand firmly, shifting awkwardly to accommodate the leg that was encased in a
thick plaster cast.

'Sorry you've been put through all this,' she said
loudly, gesturing with her square hands. 'I'm usually
pretty spry on my feet but this broken leg has slowed
me down an awful lot. Still, I suppose you would have
had to come up to the villa anyway, to shelter. Mr
Sterne was going to send Thomas down to you when
Dominic disappeared.'

Gina smiled faintly, not attempting to say anything,

her throat too raw to compete with the wind. At least it answered one question ... Leonard Sterne wasn't so without conscience that he could have let her stay in the bungalow during a hurricane, even if he did despise everything he thought she stood for.

'You're a naughty boy, Dominic.' Pamela Smythe was finally paying some attention to her charge. 'You had us all in an uproar!'

Gina could see that the idea appealed to Nic enormously. Silly woman, couldn't she see that she was playing right into his hands? From the expression on his father's face she guessed that Sterne was not satisfied with the companion's performance either. Where had she been when Nic slipped away to spend hours with Gina?

There was a crash, a violent vibration of the walls and Pamela Smythe screamed and pressed up against the tall man's side.

'What was that?'

'A tree, probably.' He extricated himself with difficulty from her clinging grasp. 'Please try and stay calm, Miss Smythe. We should be safe enough here.'

Gina sat down on the other couch, opposite the stoic Aileen Hamilton, relieved that the noise level obviated the need for conversation. Nic sat beside her, still holding her hand tightly, and Gina willed him some of her own small store of courage. Thomas and Liana sat down at the huge, pale dining-table and played cards. They looked concerned at some of the loudest vibrations but not unduly frightened, and Gina took heart from their apparent confidence in the villa's stability. She admired Aileen Hamilton for being able to knit, although from her frequent grimaces and exasperated movements Gina guessed there might be more dropped stitches than knitting, but the needles moved stubbornly. Here was a practical woman, Gina sensed, who would have a great deal of patience with Nic's special needs ... motherly and yet, as her

behaviour now proved, not one to try and force a
child's confidence.

Pamela Smythe was quite a different kettle of fish,
although it was unfair to judge her in such trying
circumstances. From her make-up and clothes Gina
thought that she was probably used to much more
civilised surroundings. Not the type who would enjoy
hunting through tropical bush in search of a truant
child. She probably also screamed at spiders.

Afraid as she was, Gina had to bite her lip to stop
herself grinning at the woman's antics. She constantly
sought Leo Sterne's reassurance about their safety and
he could barely conceal his impatience. If she had ever
thought that the companion had been chosen for her
looks rather than her competence here was the rebuttal.

'Why don't you have a drink, Miss Smythe, it might
help you relax,' she saw him tell her curtly at one point.
He poured a large brandy and glared at Gina as he
glimpsed her poorly hidden amusement. His eyes
flickered down to his son, who had stretched his legs
out on the couch and buried his face in Gina's lap. Her
hand stroked his hair as she felt fatigue catch up with
him and his body teeter on the edge of sleep. Flame
licked out of the yellow eyes and singed Gina's skin.
She jerked her eyes away to meet the thoughtful gaze of
Aileen Hamilton.

It was a strange night, a weird combination of
boredom and fear. The noise was unlike anything that
Gina had ever experienced, almost on the level of a
physical assault, battering her tired brain until she felt
almost seasick with the illusion of motion inside her
head. There were distant tearing, crashing sounds in
other parts of the house but the heavy wooden double
doors of the dining-room scarcely shook and stood
steadfast throughout the tempest.

The brandy didn't calm Pamela Smythe so Leo
Sterne gave her another, and another, callously pouring
liquor into her until she slid into a half-stupor next to

her colleague. Then, to Gina's unease, he settled on the other side of Aileen Hamilton and stared broodingly at his son. Heaven knew what he was thinking but whatever it was, it wasn't pleasant. He looked as if he was pondering some unpalatable decision and Gina's arm tightened automatically around Nic, as if he could protect her from some nameless threat issued by his father.

It felt like forty hours, but was more like four, by the time nature's lethal force had spent itself and they were all ordered off to bed to snatch a few hours' sleep before welcome daylight. Thomas reported that most of the bedrooms were undamaged and helped Aileen Hamilton to swing along the hall on her crutches while Leo Sterne manhandled an incapable redhead. Gina was given the room she had changed in and, after finding out she was next door to Nic and reassuring him that she would see him in the morning, she fell into a deep, drugged sleep.

She was awoken by Liana throwing open the shutters on the long windows and letting in a flood of sunlight.

'Sorry to disturb you, Virginia,' she said in her beautiful English. 'But I wanted to get everyone's breakfast out of the way before I start cleaning up.'

Gina struggled upright in the big bed, blinking against the strong light. 'That's OK,' she husked painfully.

'Are you all right? You sound terrible,' Liana frowned.

Gina touched her throat above the open neck of the shirt which she had kept on and the Fijian girl said with open dismay,

'Oh, I'm sorry, I didn't realise ... Mr Sterne didn't say——' She collected herself and grinned in a way that wasn't at all offensive. 'I'm making it worse with all my stuttering, aren't I? Look, I brought you a tray ... if you wouldn't mind returning it to the kitchen when you've finished. It's all cold, I'm afraid, because the generator shed was damaged, but we should get power later on in the day. Usually we have girls up from the village to help when there are guests, but things are going to be a bit disorganised for a few days.'

Gina smiled her assent, her mouth watering at the sight of the thin slices of rock melon, avocado and mango and the honeyed curve of a croissant. There was a tall glass of juice too, which she drank thirstily.

'Mmm, that's delicious, what is it?' It definitely lubricated her dry throat.

'Passion fruit and orange. You don't have to get up right away, but if you wouldn't mind keeping an eye out for Nic. He's been asking for you and Pam is so hung over I don't think she dares try to crawl out of bed.'

'How bad is it?' Gina nodded towards the window.

'I've seen worse. We lost a bit of the kitchen roof and some windows, and two of the rooms are rain-damaged, but this place is pretty well as hurricane-proof as you can get. Mr Sterne lost his yacht—it's washing up in pieces on the beach.'

'What about the village?' asked Gina, thinking cynically that Mr Sterne could afford to buy himself a dozen replacement yachts without too much hardship.

'Only one person got hurt—not badly—and the houses were knocked around a bit but luckily the village is pretty well protected on that side of the island. News over the radio has Fiji a real mess, though. Several people dead and hundreds homeless.' She shrugged. 'Cyclones are something we just have to learn to live with. Now, I'd better rush. I'll see you later.'

Gina finished her breakfast and went to wash her face with cold water in the adjoining bathroom, amazed that lack of sleep hadn't affected her look of tanned healthiness. Her hair had gone wild though, in the humidity, and sprang up around her face in a tangle of curls. She found a comb in the cabinet and managed to remove the tangles but not the curls so she rooted around and found a stray cord that would do as a ribbon. With her black tresses controlled into a frantic ponytail she went through an abbreviated form of her vocal exercises, relieved to find no trace of last night's soreness. Then it was to the chest to find something to wear. There was no sign of her wet clothes and she could hardly stay in the creased and crumpled shirt. To her dismay there was nothing else with a collar on it and the best she was able to do was a plain blue crew-neck T-shirt. She donned it gloomily, along with the cotton trousers she had draped over a chair, and was just about to leave the room when Nic bounced in.

They greeted each other with smiles and Gina noticed that he was wearing small hearing aids almost concealed by his thick dark hair. Wisely she didn't comment and let him lead her to the kitchen where she insisted on helping Liana cope with the breakfast things before allowing Nic to drag her outside.

It was as if a giant hand had flattened the surrounding bush. There were branches and rocks, seaweed and other debris piled up against the concrete walls of the villa.

Liana says it will all grow again soon. Things grow fast in the hot sun, Nic signed to her, enjoying her horrified expression.

'I wonder how my poor bungalow got on?' Gina said, raising her voice slightly. Nic frowned at her uncertainly for a moment when she made no attempt to sign, then shrugged.

You can't go yet, I want to show you my room. He signed firmly and she went thoughtfully back into the cool interior of the villa with him. He had got the gist of what she had said, even though he had been watching her hands expectantly instead of her lips, so with the aids he *could* hear, though how much she couldn't tell.

Nic took her on a tour of the villa, excepting his father's room which he avoided with as much relief as

Gina did. She saw no sign of her folio, which meant that Leo Sterne *did* have it, and she didn't dare leave without it.

Thus it was that she was still at the villa for lunch, a meal that proved to be as harrowing as she had expected. She had gone to her room and loosened her hair around her shoulders as best she could, but the scars still flashed out like a beacon. Sure enough they drew comment. As soon as she sat down at the table a wan Pamela Smythe lifted a heavy head and blurted out,

'Good heavens, how awful! What happened to your neck?'

Instantly all eyes were on her exposed throat and Gina felt her scalp tighten in agonised anticipation of parading her flaw for all to exclaim over. No matter how often she faced the reaction, it never failed to land a blow upon a secret wound.

'An operation,' she grated bluntly, knowing that she was drawing attention to her ugly voice, conscious of the man standing at the head of the table, his eyes narrowed on her stiff face.

'Are you convalescing here?' Aileen Hamilton asked, smoothing over the awkward pause as she accepted a plate of chilled soup from Liana. Nic edged his chair closer to Gina's, thereby managing to hide himself from his father's view as he sat down.

Gina looked down at her soup with a smile that she hoped would be taken as acquiescence but Leo Sterne wouldn't let her get away with it. As he spread his napkin in his lap he drawled,

'I thought you claimed to be working.'

'Oh, are you a writer then?' Aileen asked pleasantly.

'Yes, Miss Bennett, tell us what you do all day,' the lion rumbled sarcastically.

'I draw,' Gina said through clenched teeth.

Leo Sterne laughed sceptically and spoons which had dug into the fragrant seafood bisque paused as the other women sensed the sudden undercurrents.

'So you're the reason for Nic's new interest in art,' Aileen Hamilton plunged gently into the silence, unknowingly annoying her employer even further with her revelation. 'I wondered why he suddenly started drawing all over his stories. He's improved, too. Have you been helping him?'

'I've let him use some of my paper and pencils,' Gina admitted, feeling waves of antagonism flow down from the end of the table. 'He's quite a quick study at drawing. Aren't you, Nic?' She turned to him and repeated her words. He stared at her but from the rigid set of his shoulders she saw that he either didn't hear, or was pretending not to. She signed her words to him with an uncritical smile, so that he relaxed slightly and nodded.

'You can sign, what an incredible coincidence!' Aileen exclaimed. 'How did you come to learn? Oh, of course, how silly of me, I suppose because of your throat?'

Gina nodded, crumbling a roll nervously.

'No wonder Nic has taken to you.' The tutor seemed only approving as she looked from Nic to the dark, strained-looking young woman next to him. 'He's so very aware of being different, it's good for him to discover that everyone is different in one way or another, that nobody is perfect in every way.' She pulled a comical face. 'I tell him that my eyesight is weak and I have to wear glasses but he claims that doesn't count.'

She had signed, too, so that Nic wouldn't feel isolated from the conversation that he couldn't pick up audibly and he and Gina exchanged a look of secret understanding. Until you had experienced what it was like to be completely and irrevocably isolated from most of mankind you couldn't begin to understand the loneliness.

Actually deafness, for a child, was a painless thing. Gina knew from her experiences at the pre-school centre for deaf children that it was usually the parents who suffered initially. Only when the child began to develop intellectually did he begin to understand that he was handicapped. Obviously this was the stage that Nic was at—the more he struggled to overcome his deafness the more aware he was of its restrictions. And his hearing aid, perhaps he hated that as the symbol of his deafness, revealing it to the world as her scars had revealed Gina's handicap. She had explained to him about her accident, about the years of silence, about the miracle operation, and oddly he seemed to regard her 'cure' with as much satisfaction as if *he* had been the surgeon, not resenting that her 'difference' was now only superficial. She knew what it was like, she had lived it, and that was enough for him.

'So, Miss Bennett, you're an artist,' the cold voice sliced into her thoughts. 'Do you sell any of these great works of art? Or perhaps you *give* them away to friends.' Implying she was dilettante if not downright untalented.

'I'm not an artist, I'm an illustrator,' she replied rigidly and jumped when Aileen suddenly set down her spoon with a thump.

'Goodness! Nic calls you Gina. Are you Gina Bennett?' Gina smiled weakly at her shocked exclamation. 'Mr Sterne quite put me off, introducing you as Virginia. Goodness, I feel I know you well—I just love your books! Nic has had me read one over and over to him the last week or so. Gina Bennett! What a lovely and unexpected surprise!'

CHAPTER FIVE

SHE was the only one who seemed to think so. Pamela Smythe, greener by the minute, was making a major effort just to stay at the table and Leo Sterne merely watched sourly as Aileen brimmed over with enthusiastic questions.

Gina fended her off with a mixture of embarrassment and secret pride. If it hadn't been for Leo Sterne's silent glower she would have responded naturally to the praise. What was he annoyed about now, for heaven's sake? That she wasn't an idle, useless socialite like her sisters?

Towards the end of the meal, she forced herself to address him calmly. 'Do you ... have you got my satchel? I'd like to go back to the bungalow as soon as possible.'

'It'll be a wasted trip, Raymond took the roof off.'

'Raymond?' Gina gave him a darkling look. Had he used one of his employees to ensure she wouldn't be able to stay on the island?

'The cyclone,' he replied drily, reading the look.

'Oh. The roof? But all my things!' she said in dismay.

'Thomas and I went down there at first light. We did manage to salvage a few of your belongings but the place is water-logged. It'll be weeks before it's habitable again,' he said, hatefully smug, before switching his attention to Nic. 'Perhaps you'd like to come down to the plantation with me later and help with the clearing up, Dom. Thomas says that nearly every tree and bush was uprooted. I don't think there'll be any Paradise avocados or pawpaws for sale this year.'

'That'll be fun, won't it, Nic?' prompted Aileen Hamilton when there was no reply.

I want to stay with Gina, Nic signed sullenly to his tutor.

Leo Sterne shrugged, but when he rose from the table he said smoulderingly to Gina, 'Come to my office when you've finished, Miss Bennett. There are one or two things I'd like to say to you.'

And there are a lot of things I'd like to say to *you*, Gina thought acidly as she helped Liana with the lunch dishes, ignoring her protests that she had helped with breakfast.

'I thought you artistic types were supposed to be terribly selfish and disorganised,' the Fijian girl grinned. 'We've had one or two writers staying here and oh boy!' she flipped her hands expressively.

'Women writers?' asked Gina casually as she wiped her hands on the tea towel.

'Of course women, Mr Sterne is strictly conservative in that direction,' Liana said, her dark eyes twinkling.

'Well, I found that not having a voice does wonders for one's organisational abilities,' Gina said, regretting her brief moment of curiosity. 'Everything has to be thought out very well in advance, because you can't just pick up a telephone and order something you forgot or ask a stranger for instructions or directions without indulging in a game of charades.' It had been one of the first lessons, and the hardest, that she had learnt after the accident: and she had realised slowly, over a period of months, just how much she had taken for granted in her life. It wasn't her wealth or social position which had gained her so much acceptance, it was her ability to fit into the expected mould. Once she no longer fitted it she no longer 'belonged', making her wonder whether she ever really had.

'I've got to go and see your father now, Nic,' Gina explained to her shadow as they left the kitchen.

His face set. 'Is he going to send you away?'

'If the bungalow is wrecked I can't very well stay

there, can I?' she said gently. 'And that's the storm's fault, not your father's.'

'You can stay here, with me,' he said stubbornly.

Gina shook her head involuntarily, appalled at the prospect of living in the lion's den.

'It's *him*, isn't it,' Nic burst out. 'You don't like me any more because of *him*.'

'Of course I still like you, Nic,' she said, feeling guilty that she was allowing her negative feelings towards his father to influence her. 'We're friends, nothing can change that.'

'*He* can,' Nic's face twisted. '*He* doesn't like me having friends. He'll make you go away, I know he will. I *hate* him!'

He ran down the hallway and Gina let him go, upset that she seemed to be exacerbating an already bad situation. Perhaps it was for the best that she was forced to leave Paradise; she had been allowing Nic to develop an emotional dependence on her because it had satisfied some need in herself to be wanted, rather than because it was best for him.

Disquietened she set her reluctant feet in the direction Liana had indicated that Sterne's office lay.

She wondered whether her voice would stand up to another verbal clash with him. It seemed that almost every time they met he was in the grip of some violent emotion.

She remembered their first meeting, when she had had no voice at all. He had stood in the doorway of the blue-and-white bedroom, all tawny eyes and hair and skin, like a full-grown lion and every bit as ferocious. Gina had been so stunned by his sheer male presence that at first she had hardly noticed the sobbing fair-haired woman in the crook of his arm.

Gina had clutched the sheet against her, painfully trying to cope with the first and last hangover of her young life, and the realisation that for some reason she was naked except for flimsy underwear, and that Niven lay beside her, similarly undressed. She had no recollection beyond embarking on a bottle of champagne—or two—with him the night before, happily believing that after the champagne he would produce a ring. That would be just like Niven—funny, secretive, terribly romantic—his manner so different from the painfully awkward approaches of family friends who wouldn't see beyond the handicap to the *person*.

It was only when she caught some of the sobbing woman's words and saw the glitter of a gold band as she raised her hands to her agonised face that Gina had realised the truth. This woman, this woman was Niven's *wife*; and the bed they were in was their marriage bed! He was married! All the time that he had been taking her out, making a game of concealing their relationship from her family, seeking out tiny, out-of-the-way restaurants for romantic assignations, allowing her to fall in *love* with him, all the time he was *married!*

She had turned her eyes, wide and wounded, to him, but Niven was staring with an alien, hard defiance at his wife and at the man who now stepped forward, putting the tearful woman behind him.

'If you value that pretty face of yours, Niven, you'll get out while you can,' he had grated with searing contempt, his eyes flicking over Gina's raw skin in a way that made her flinch. 'And take this little tramp with you.'

Gina had put her hand on Niven's arm, silently pleading for him to explain. Surely she hadn't been so drunk . . . no, there was no stiffness or soreness and she didn't believe that Niven would have gone so far as to take her while she was unconscious. Up until now he had been quite satisfied with romantic kisses.

'No need to get so uptight, Leo. We got a bit high last night, that's all. Virginia was about to leave, weren't you, darling?'

The name had been like a bucket of icy water, adding

to her frozen shock. Niven *never* called her Virginia, knowing that was what her mother always called her, that it belonged to that *other* girl, the one she might have become if fate hadn't intervened so savagely. It was Gina, always; softly, tenderly. She had tried to sign her bewilderment but Niven had caught her hands and disguised the movement, and behind the tawny giant there had been another sob as Niven's wife fled back down the curving staircase.

The thick, threatening silence had been broken by Niven's nervous laugh. 'It won't happen again, old man, I swear.'

A lethal smile: the lion in motion. He had strode to the side of the bed and wrenched Niven up by the hair.

'You're right,' he had snarled, close to his captive's reddened ear. 'Because, as of this moment, you and my sister are no longer husband and wife. Since you so conveniently eloped to Mexico to marry, divorce should be just as convenient. And if you ever try to come near Kathy again, or make any protests or demands, I'll beat that face you depend on so much to a bloody pulp. Understand!'

Unbelievably, Niven had managed a peculiar smile. Only later had Gina realised why—because he had just achieved his goal, and was intent on consolidating his victory.

'What's it worth to you, Leo? A quiet divorce?' he had taunted.

Almost casually Leonard Sterne had steadied his brother-in-law's head and used his other hand to deliver a stunning backhand blow across the face. Blood had gushed from Niven's nose and mouth as he was shoved viciously back on to the bed, Gina had drawn a sharp breath as she saw that he was still smiling as he tried to staunch the flow with the silk sheet.

'It's worth nothing to me,' the other man had told him savagely. 'But *everything* to you. You know what I'm capable of, Niven. Just make sure that you and your little home-wrecking playmate don't *ever* cross my path again!'

'Don't worry, Virginia knows the score,' Niven had said with a cruel carelessness that had sent humiliation shivering across Gina's skin as the leonine head was thrown back and the eyes slitted to survey her with a mixture of sensual appreciation and contempt.

'I guessed that from her silence. But I wonder whether, in a week's time, you'll think that she was worth it, *ex*-brother-in-law.'

Gina's humiliation had been consumed in a sudden burst of fury against male brutality. She had been vilely used and now she was being insulted for her naivety. She had risen from the bed, stiff with angry pride, and stalked across to the open bathroom door. There she had paused to direct a look of proud and fiery hatred at her tormentors. Niven's blue eyes had slid away, but the lion had traded her look for look.

Slamming the door violently behind her Gina had slumped by the marble bathtub, her proud facade splintered into tiny fragments. Niven had lied. Worse, she knew now that the reason he had sought her out after a brief meeting at one of her mother's parties was *because* of her lack of voice, not in spite of it. He had wanted a silent dupe. And she had been disgustingly grateful for his attention, lapping up his lies about how she didn't need speech to fascinate him, how her intelligence and talent conquered all barriers, how he enjoyed being with her. Lies, all lies. He had probably been bored to tears, as well as embarrassed by her scars. He had never touched her neck when he kissed her and had subtly encouraged her obsession with high collars by carefully directing his eyes away whenever he caught a glimpse of the red ridges.

Gina had felt sick, the cold floor of the bathroom rising up to meet her fiery face. Why? Why had he done it? He must have known that she was falling in love with him. Why? She had shaken with silent, soul-shattering sobs, aching for a voice to howl out her pain, to cry like any other wounded creature, but her agony was locked away inside her. Up until now she had been able to convince herself that she had accepted the fact she would never speak again, but the knife in her heart had ripped out all the old, fiercely denied hopes.

Standing before Leonard Sterne's door Gina tried to pluck up the courage to knock. She had felt even more besmirched, later, when Niven had tried to explain why he had done what he had, and she had never seen him again after that night. For a long time nothing had mattered. Five long, bitter weeks later she had learned of a new technique for reconstructive surgery on the larynx and had gone into the operating theatre not really caring whether she lived or died. Six months more of compulsory silence had followed before she was allowed to exercise her vocal chords and during that time she had penned *The Long Silence* and had sworn that no man would ever, ever hurt her that way again.

The first thing she saw on entering the room was the bed and coming so close on the heels of vile memory it was like a blow in the chest. Gina's skin heated and it was a moment before her vision cleared sufficiently for her to see Leonard Sterne seated behind a large desk beside the open window.

Swallowing, Gina managed to walk on wobbly legs over to the desk, trying to angle her head so that she couldn't see the distracting bed. She came to an abrupt halt as she saw that the papers he was so intently studying were her drawings and that her folio lay limply beside his desk. Not completely limp, though. She could see the cardboard carton inside. He couldn't have looked further than the pictures. She collapsed into the nearest chair with relief.

'How long have you been doing this kind of thing?' he shot at her suddenly, looking up.

'A . . . about two and a half years,' said Gina huskily,

putting one elbow on the arm of her chair and moving her hand in front of her throat self-consciously.

'Why?' he probed, hard-faced.

'Because I like doing it, because I'm good at it.' Because I desperately needed a sense of purpose, of self-worth, she could have gone on ... something to replace the nothingness. If she hadn't been afraid of her whole life being sucked into a silent void she might never have discovered her latent talent for drawing, but once she had she had worked at it feverishly, to the exclusion of everything else. Until Niven.

'You *are* good,' he admitted moodily, the surprise of his discovery still lingering in his voice.

'And I'm going to be even better,' she said defiantly.

'Confident, aren't you?' he accused.

She shrugged, sensing it annoyed him. 'I have the sales to prove it.'

'Why didn't you tell me?' He got to the source of his annoyance—the fact that he had been wrong.

'You didn't ask me!' she snapped. 'You're so good at assumptions. Anyway, you probably wouldn't have believed me if I *had* told you.'

'Are these for publication?' he infuriated her by ignoring the opening for an apology.

'Yes.'

'You've captured Dom perfectly,' he took her off guard by saying, his finger tracing a picture of Jao fishing in his island lagoon.

'He was easy to draw,' she summoned defensive sarcasm, 'and if you're going to accuse me of exploiting him I can tell you that I paid him for posing.'

'And what kind of payment do I get?' he asked blandly, turning one of the drawings of the magician towards her.

'I . . . that wasn't deliberate,' she denied hoarsely. 'He just turned out that way.' She leaned forward to gather up the pages and slide them into the stiff cover that protected them, continuing tight-lipped, 'Personally I don't think you have to worry about being recognised, but naturally I can make changes if——'

'I suppose he's a black-eyed villain who eats little children alive,' he said broodingly, watching her long-fingered hands as she tried to take the last picture from him. He held it away.

'No, he's not!' Gina leapt to the defence of her character. 'He's a magician, wild and wondrous and lord of the isle. He's supposed to inspire awe so he has to be a bit dramatic.'

'And naturally you thought of me.' He let her take the picture, watching her flush as she bent down to put the cover back in her folio and raise the hand back to her throat. The gesture irritated him.

'I told you, he just turned out that way,' she said stonily.

'I'm flattered that I live so vividly in your imagination,' he said softly. 'Is that how I appear to you ... wild and wondrous?'

Gina forced herself to ignore the speculative note he injected into the velvety voice. He just wanted her to *think* he was softening.

'You're no more that than Nic is a homeless waif, you were just the right physical type, that's all,' she said tautly, seeing the faint gleam of humour die away completely at her mention of his son.

'So what was all that Borelli business about? That's not your pen-name, according to Miss Hamilton.'

She tucked in her chin, prepared for the worst. 'I ... I'm trying something new this time. I ... my agent suggested the name.'

'What exactly was that operation for? Was there something the matter with your vocal cords?'

She glared at him silently, unable to keep up with his rapid changes of subject, or to see where it was all leading.

'I thought you'd decided I'd slit my throat to have an

excuse to worm my way into Nic's confidence, and thereby into yours.'

'Don't be bloody stupid,' he growled at her, a faint colour touching the broad cheekbones.

'My vocal cords are nothing to do with you,' Gina went on belligerently. 'I shall be quite happy to get off this island and have nothing whatever more to do with you and your insults and your blind prejudices!'

'Well, you'll just have to suffer me a little longer.' He smiled at her unpleasantly.

'What do you mean? You said the bungalow was uninhabitable.'

'So it is. But the villa's not.'

Gina couldn't believe what he was suggesting. 'I'm not going to stay *here*!' she exploded quietly.

He leaned back in his chair, all golden insolence. 'And how do you plan to leave?'

'I should have thought you'd be happy to fly me off.'

'I've loaned the jet to the Fijian Government to help with the airlifting of people and construction materials on the main islands. I would say that for the next couple of weeks most available aircraft will be similarly tied up.'

'By boat, then,' she snapped.

He shrugged muscular shoulders. He was wearing a designer T-shirt with stretch jeans this morning, and the butter-yellow fabric enhanced the golden-boy image and pleaded with the artist in her to admire his symmetry. 'It could be some time before services are back to normal. Certainly this week's supply-boat won't be calling, and most of the village boats were sunk ... not to mention my own.'

'Then how in the hell do you expect me to leave ... swim?' she demanded sarcastically. He raised his eyebrows in silence and Gina's whole body tightened. 'You can't expect me to believe that you *want* me to stay.'

'No. But Dominic does.'

Gina was incredulous. 'And you let Nic decide who stays and goes?'

'In this instance I really don't have any choice.' The insolence fell away and an implacable hardness entered his eyes. It wasn't just a cruel game, he really meant it! 'Dominic doesn't take to people easily, but when he does he's very intense about it. He thinks he already has plenty of reasons to hate me, I don't want to hand him another.'

'So you're going to make me stay here ... until what?' Gina demanded.

His eyes flickered over her. 'Until he discovers that his idol has feet of clay.'

'What makes you think he will?' Gina bristled.

His smile was filled with a humourless certainty. 'Living twenty-four hours a day with someone is quite different from visiting. You may have tolerated his disruptive presence while you were using him for your illustrations, but I don't think it'll take you long to tire of Nic's constant demands for attention and show your true colours when you're with him day after day.'

'Maybe it's *you* who don't see me as I really am,' she said huskily, on the offensive.

'It won't take you long to get bored with his juvenile company,' he said confidently. 'And start yearning for the bright lights again.'

'I've been here for a month without getting bored,' she pointed out furiously.

'But you've been working. Those illustrations look pretty well finished. We'll see how sweet and sympathetic you can stay when you've got nothing to do but dance attendance on one selfish and self-centred little boy.'

'How can you talk about your son that——'

'Because he *is* my son!' He leant forward on the desk and pushed the words at her. 'I see him as he is, not through rose-coloured spectacles. He's too used to being given everything he wants on his own terms. He's been spoiled rotten and it's time it stopped.'

'And this is your way of stopping it!'

'Yes.' His eyes glittered. 'Once he sees that I'm not going to allow him to use you as a weapon to manipulate me he might begin to regard me with a little respect. And respect is something I can build on.'

Gina drew a breath. 'And you accused *me* of using him,' she whispered. 'You're going to use *me*, aren't you? You're going to use me to get close to your own son.'

'I can't lose, can I?' His smile twisted. 'If your behaviour doesn't succeed in alienating him it makes no difference. While you're here the three of us will be like *that*.' He held up a strong, rock-steady hand, the three middle fingers intertwined. 'Wherever you go, I'll go, and if necessary I'll walk across your back to him. He *will* accept me.'

The tight, terse phrasing seethed with an animal frustration that Gina sensed he was longing to set free. It frightened her, yet at the same time it made her curious as to its source.

'But why? Why should you have to force him to accept you? What kind of father have you been that he should have reasons to hate you?' she asked shakily.

He didn't answer for a moment, as if fighting with himself as to whether to tell her at all. Then he shrugged.

'No father at all, not for the past six years. I didn't have custody and my—Nic's mother made a mockery out of the visiting rights we had agreed upon. Dom has only been living with me for the past six months.'

Had his ex-wife died? Or remarried? Gina didn't dare ask. But the brief explanation answered a lot of questions, as well as shattering some of her harsh preconceptions of Leonard Sterne. She fought against the temptation to soften towards him.

'Why can't you approach him honestly? Talk to him about it?' she said.

'I will, when the time is right. When he's ready to

listen and old enough to understand. But he's hiding behind his deafness, shutting me out. And I won't let him continue. I won't let him think he can beat me.'

'It's not a contest——' Gina choked.

'Oh, but it is. Dom's made it into a contest, perhaps even a test of some kind, who knows what's going around in that stubborn head of his? So I'll play his game . . . for a while. He's been winning for the last six months because I didn't have the time to stand and fight, but this is where I make my stand. By the time he and I leave Paradise we'll be father and son—in every sense.'

'But for now you want my help.' Gina's words intruded into some private battleground, for the head reared, and the sensuous mouth thinned.

'Not help. I don't need your help. All I want is your presence, human nature will do the rest.'

'What about Pamela Smythe? What about all the time that Nic spends with Miss Hamilton?' Gina tried to deflect him.

'I'll cut his lessons to a couple of hours. They're not important at this stage, and he's not co-operating. As for the Smythe woman, she's been a complete waste of time. She's used to working with much younger children. She doesn't know how to reach him any more than I do . . . can,' he corrected himself quickly. 'I'll get rid of her as soon as I can.'

'I won't let you do it,' Gina whispered and his face changed with startling suddenness as he stood up, curving into lines of triumphant amusement.

'Won't you, Virginia?'

Then she heard what he had seen. Nic moving up beside her, eyes fixed on her flushed and angry face, bursting with the need to know.

'You're going away,' he said flatly.

'No, she's not. I've asked her to stay,' said Leo Sterne loudly, his hands at his sides. The small dark face jolted in shock to the tawny, waiting one. 'She can stay as long as she wants to,' he continued, looking deep into his son's eyes for the first time in months.

'Gina?' The boy turned on a tiny whisper of hope and Gina felt her throat catch at the look of shy joy he revealed.

She looked over her head at the man beyond, who was making no attempt to hide his satisfaction. 'You——'

'Tell him, Virginia,' he urged softly out of his son's hearing. 'Tell him that you don't want to stay. Tell him you have better things to do. Start his education.'

'I should do just that,' she said lightly, hardly moving her lips.

'Didn't I say you were a heartless bitch?' he taunted.

'You'll think that anyway.'

'Change my mind.' He laid out the soft, golden challenge before her with utter contempt. He didn't really care, or believe that she ever really could. In spite of what he had learned about her in the last twelve hours he still thought that she was tarred with the same brush as her sisters.

'Gina?' Whatever she thought of his father, she couldn't bear to wipe away that shy joy. She gritted her teeth and smiled.

'I'm staying; for a while.'

The triumph on Nic's young face was a mirror image of his father's. 'With me? In my room? I've got two beds, you can sleep with me!'

There was a hiss behind him and Leo Sterne stepped forward, taking up a commanding stance next to Gina, aligning himself with her.

'Virginia will have her own room, where she was last night. It's right next to you. But she needs space to work.'

'She can work in my room,' the boy protested stubbornly.

'She still needs a private place for herself,' came the unwavering reply. 'Everyone needs somewhere to be alone, to think. Virginia. You. Me,' linking them all together. 'Now, why don't you go and tell Liana that we have another house guest for a while?'

Nic trotted out with alacrity after a single beaming smile at Gina.

'That's the first time he's spoken directly to me, or actually listened to what I had to say,' the tall man gloated, his eyes on the door his son had left open. He gave a savage little laugh of satisfaction. 'I would have done it eventually, my own way. But I'll take any short cut that's offered.' He looked jubilantly into Gina's wide, stormy eyes. 'Even you, Virginia Bennett.'

'I hope for your sake that you get what you want, Leo Sterne, instead of what you deserve,' she hissed at him and walked out, torn by conflicting fury and admiration for what he was doing. She could understand, given that minuscule glimpse into the strains of the past, what it was that was driving him but it didn't make her like him, or the situation he was forcing them into, any better. She had fought against exactly this kind of involvement for she was afraid that there was every chance she could end up *caring* about the outcome of this father-son conflict. Curiosity was the first step to caring, and already it was nibbling at her attempted indifference.

CHAPTER SIX

LEO STERNE propped himself up on one elbow, shifting his body to a more comfortable postition in the warm sand so that he could watch the woman and child splashing at the water's edge.

The jealousy was still there, getting in the way, but it was now intermingled with other emotions ... not the least of them dismay. Virginia Bennett had confounded all his expectations. Not only had she *not* tired of babysitting Dominic all day every day, she had seemed to thrive on it. And Dominic was equally tireless in his devotion.

He saw the boy flick some sand into his companion's face and be admonished with rapid hand movements. She wasn't afraid, as Leo was, of being hated for denying the boy something, or correcting his behaviour, and Dom seemed to take her frowns and reprovals in his stride. Damn it, she had charmed everyone—except Leo. He was forced to sit by and watch his household fall under her peculiar spell. Even Aileen Hamilton, who up until now had been the only one who was able to do anything with Dominic, had nothing but praise for her temporary colleague, particularly since she had elicited the information that Gina had worked among deaf children for a while herself, on a strictly amateur basis.

'It was more for my benefit than for theirs,' the dark-eyed young woman had admitted huskily at dinner one night.

'In what way for your benefit?' Leo had asked and she had turned her head to look at him, the wariness that so annoyed him showing on her face.

'They helped me discover what children like best

about my pictures, they had no qualms about criticising anything they didn't like. And . . .'

'And?' he had prompted her when her voice had sunk to a halt, the voice that had first irritated him but now seemed to rasp along under his skin.

She had shrugged. 'And when I was first learning signing they were great teachers.'

He sensed that there was a great deal more to it than she was saying, but not even Aileen Hamilton's subtle interrogation could make her expand on her statement in more than vague terms.

They were kicking water at each other now, and laughing. In spite of the stilted relationship between the two adults, Leo had to admit that she had been surprisingly co-operative in trying to ease the situation between him and Dominic. She hadn't overtly done anything, but her mere presence had served to defuse some of the tenseness in the atmosphere. Father and son hadn't progressed any closer to each other, but neither had things regressed. With the woman between them they could both pretend to a casual indifference while surreptitiously observing each other.

He watched her bend, the black hair falling forward, sparkling with drops of water like stars caught in a midnight sky. He didn't know whether it was false modesty or perversity that had made her refuse to wear any of the skimpy bikinis back at the villa. Perhaps she knew that the pareu was infinitely more sexy, he thought cynically, making her look like a dark-skinned pagan. Yet he couldn't claim that she played on her sexuality. On the contrary she seemed almost uncomfortable with it, but that had to be a ploy of some kind. He couldn't believe that any woman with a body and a background such as hers could be sexually uncertain.

Leo's hand clenched around a fistful of sand, his eyes caressing her long legs. That was another complication. Sex. Her company was proving to be far more of a distraction than he had bargained for. She aroused an unwelcome hunger in him that it was going to be difficult to appease or deny. How did he square it with his conscience—wanting to bed the woman who had finally destroyed Kathy's admittedly shaky marriage? Even more impossible to swallow was the thought that Niven had tasted her first.

They were coming back up the beach now and Leo watched with resignation as their laughter died. He hadn't felt such an outsider since those early courting years with Cynthia, before he had made enough money to satisfy her family's fastidiousness about his working-class background. Better for them both if he never had . . . but then there would not have been Dominic.

He watched through half-lowered lids as Gina rubbed his son down, remembering the way he had offered to rub her down when she had shivered like a half-drowned rat. His mouth curved. Her temper hadn't quite disguised her embarrassment. It gave him a prick of satisfaction to think that she was still capable of being embarrassed. Perhaps it meant she wasn't entirely beyond salvage.

'Water warm?' he asked her, as she patted her own legs dry. Her towel was beside his because Dom didn't want to be next to his father but he noticed that she made sure there was a good stretch of sand between them. Could it be that she sensed his interest and was disturbed by it? Good. He wanted to disturb her. In fact, he was beginning to think that he might want more of her than she would ever be able to give.

'Lovely,' she murmured, looking at him in surprise, her thick lashes dropping when she saw that his expression matched the lazy warmth that had been in his voice. He wondered what she was thinking. The pareu twisted across her hips as she spread out her towel. Child-bearing hips, he thought, broad and suggestive of a secret strength.

He felt the slight stirring of his body but made no

attempt to hide it, watching her face. Her eyes flickered at him briefly as she sat down and she looked away hurriedly, but the ear he could see was scarlet. He shifted his legs and she nearly leapt out of her skin. He grinned, suddenly beginning to enjoy himself. Perhaps it was about time that he and the contradictory Miss Bennett came to an understanding.

'Don't be embarrassed, it's a perfectly natural reaction,' he said wickedly.

'What is?' she snapped, not turning around, but her hand moved up to tug nervously at the knot above her breasts. For a moment he was taken aback by her demand for frankness, then he realised with further amusement that she thought he was talking about *her* reaction. His eyes lingered on the hand that hid the profile of her breast from him.

'Actually I was talking about *my* reaction,' he teased her. 'You're very lovely and very skimpily dressed, and I can't control a certain amount of curiosity.'

She rummaged in her beach-bag, looking flustered and startlingly young and he felt his curiosity intensify.

'Would you like me to put that on your back?' he asked as she unscrewed a bottle of sunscreen.

'I only need it on my face,' she said hastily. 'My skin's got enough of a tan to handle a few hours' sunlight.'

'Not this kind of sunlight.' He indicated the searingly-blue sky. 'You still need some protection.'

'I'll do it——' she tried to get back the bottle he had snatched deftly.

'And let Dominic think that you don't like me to touch you? What kind of example is that?' he asked cunningly.

She looked at Nic who was watching them carefully. She could see that he was puzzled as to why she seemed so willing to talk to the enemy, and sensed an uncertainty in him. Leo had accompanied them on jaunts all over the island in the past three days, had been so casual, relaxed and unthreatening in the face of even the most anti-social of behaviour that Nic couldn't but be comparing this tolerant, lazy lion with the ferocious beast of his imagination. Gina was feeling a little puzzled herself. He had even stopped making sarcastic little asides to her and glowering at her every time she and Nic exchanged a friendly glance.

'I ... all right,' she said reluctantly. 'You put your hat on, Nic, and then we can put some lotion on you, too.' She signed as she spoke, since it had proved useless to make him wear his hearing aid down to the beach. Already two had been damaged and Gina wouldn't have put it past Nic to deliberately dunk them in the sea to get rid of them.

'Why don't you like wearing it?' she had asked him one morning.

'They hurt my head,' he had said sullenly.

'Too noisy?' she said sympathetically, knowing that some children did find them tiresome and difficult to adjust to. But if he didn't use it he would miss so much. Aileen Hamilton had told her that Nic's hearing loss was quite substantial, but not the result of a birth defect.

'He got measles with complications when he was five,' she had explained. 'Actually no one realised that he had a hearing loss ... and then there was a misdiagnosis—quite common in young deaf children when they're as withdrawn and unco-operative as Dominic.'

'I wondered why some of his speech was so clear,' Gina admitted.

'Yes,' Aileen shook her head impatiently. 'He can do and say a lot more than he lets on. His withholding is a way of controlling his life. He's very confused and I think perhaps that he has some vague idea that deafness is a punishment for something. God knows what, he won't confide in me—in anyone—but keep it in mind if he says anything odd.'

Gina had nodded, wanting to know more but half afraid of what she might find out.

She stiffened as she felt strong fingers slide across her shoulder-blades, smoothing the cream into her salty skin. Leo Sterne was the reason she was afraid. His physicality disrupted her thought processes. Why did she let him talk her into these things? She should have refused to let him touch her, but then the golden eyes would have darkened reproachfully, the pupils widen until his eyes resembled Nic's and there would be the same puzzled disillusionment there, so that she found herself automatically doing what he wanted, even though she knew he was shamelessly manipulating. The thing that unnerved her most was their enforced closeness as they passed lazy days doing all the kinds of things that a normal family might do on an island holiday. But they weren't a normal family. There was nothing normal about the situation at all ... especially her growing reaction to Leo Sterne.

Her eyes squeezed shut as the warm fingers kneaded the tense muscles on either side of her neck. Like now. She suspected that she was being given a rather sensual massage but she didn't dare say anything. What if it were only her imagination that his hands were more caressing than rubbing? And he *was* succeeding in easing away some of her stiffness. It sapped her energy, trying to remain aloof from him all the time. She had long ago given up over Nic, he had stolen a little piece of her heart with his innocent joy in her company and it would be useless to deny it. And because she wanted his joy to continue she made herself fall in with all his father's plans, knowing how much Nic's future happiness might lie in the foundations laid now for their relationship.

She sighed softly, her eyes fluttering open to see Nic frowning at her curiously. With a start she realised that her body was leaning back into the soothing, smoothing hands and she jerked away.

'Th-thank you, that's enough.'

'Pity,' came the murmur in her ear as he leaned over to return the bottle of lotion.

'Come and get some shells,' Nic ordered suddenly, not liking the funny look on Gina's face. And his father's eyes were smiling ... *his* eyes were smiling ... but not at Nic—at Gina. He didn't like *him* smiling at Gina like that.

'I want to lie down for a while,' Gina told him. In truth she would have liked to run away, but didn't think that her knees would hold her up, they felt dangerously weak. She knew it wasn't from fatigue, although the sheer physical exercise involved in keeping up with a determined seven-year-old was a bit of an eye-opener. She would never admit that to the man beside her, of course, he would just despise her all the more for being soft.

He obviously had no trouble keeping up. He looked in superb physical condition. Without looking at him Gina could see the honey-gold skin that undulated over well defined muscles and the thick golden hair that covered his arms and chest and powerful legs, hair that looked soft to the touch, a silky tangle of warmth. He seemed totally unselfconscious about his body, parading around in a variety of brief togs— yellow today—as if unaware he was nearly naked. Once he had worn a flesh-coloured pair that had almost sent Gina into a state of shock. She had actually thought he *was* naked when he rose from the water and came towards her and Nic as they arrived on the beach. She had been unable to tear her eyes away from him as he had sauntered up and bent easily to pick up his towel and he had stood before her as if he enjoyed having her stare at him with such wide-eyed curiosity. So now she tried not to notice what he was wearing ... or *not* wearing ... not wanting to pander to what was probably already an over-inflated ego where women were concerned.

'*I'll* come if you like, Nic,' his father said, wiping the

cream off his hands on the corner of his towel before signing his offer.

'I don't want to go, now.' Nic frowned his disappointment at Gina and moved away to start digging a hole in the sand with a fierceness that scattered sand in all direction.

There was a stifled sound from Leo and Gina read his tight expression.

'Give him time,' she husked softly.

'I *am* giving him time,' he gritted. 'Why won't *he* give *me* any?'

'Now you sound like Nic,' Gina responded, trying to lighten his obvious frustration.

'His name is Dominic, or Dom.' He turned on her with a glare.

'He likes me to call him Nic.'

The glare faded, to be replaced by a cynical resignation. 'Symptomatic of our relationship, wouldn't you say, that we can't even agree to call him by the same name?' He lay on his side, one hand propping up his head, the other resting comfortably on a long thigh. Gina, meeting his narrowed eyes, felt breathless. There was no aggression there now. They had a brooding, dreamy quality that seemed to search inside her.

'You can't expect miracles. It's only been a few days,' she said tentatively.

'You're a miracle. At least he doesn't run screaming out of the room any more when I walk in.'

Gina was shocked. 'Did he do that?' She instinctively turned her body towards him, even though she knew that Nic couldn't hear them talking softly, his sulky back presented to his non-attentive audience.

The golden face was dimmed with the memory. 'I suppose I can't blame him. He didn't know me. He'd been ill, was frightened by what had happened to him, and Cynthia said he'd always been a bit quiet, a loner. That's why it took so long for anyone to realise what was wrong.'

'But didn't *she* . . .' Gina stopped, appalled by the implications and certain that any moment Leo was going to realise who he was musing aloud to.

He looked out over the sharp azure curve of lagoon, flat and clear as glass and then back at Gina.

'Don't stop there. You wouldn't be human if you weren't curious.'

'I haven't been prying,' she said defensively. 'Miss Hamilton just explained how Nic came to be deaf, that's all.'

'I wasn't criticising,' he said quietly. '*Aren't* you curious?'

'I . . . a little,' Gina admitted, flushing slightly at the lie. *A lot*.

'If I tell you, will you tell me one or two things in exchange?'

'What things?' she said warily.

'Nothing about your family, or about Niven, if that's what you're worried about,' his mouth twisted derisively. 'Just a few things about yourself.' His mouth softened. 'I'm human enough to be curious, too.'

'All right,' she agreed. He probably wanted to ask about her work, or about her experience with deaf children.

'It's not particularly pleasant,' he warned her drily. 'Neither I, nor Cynthia, come out of it particularly well. Comfortable?' he mocked her attention with a teasing eyebrow. 'Then I'll begin . . .

'Cynthia's father was in publishing—that's how I got my start in the business—then I married the boss's daughter which served to confirm my success. Oh, we were in love——' as he saw Gina's expression, '—or at least we thought we were. We liked the same things, money, possessions, intellectual society—Cynthia because she was used to them and me because I wasn't. We were both ambitious and it was understood that I would build up a publishing business of my own. Cyn never objected to me working long hours or nagged me because I was hardly ever home. Quite the reverse, she was always encouraging, always busy with lunches and literary parties, the perfect supportive wife in fact.'

'Then what happened?' Gina asked, feeling a pang at the thought of Leo and his perfect wife. Was he still in love with her?

He smiled mirthlessly. 'She tried to be too perfect. She tried to combine perfect wife with perfect mother and couldn't cope.'

'You mean she had a breakdown?' Gina frowned.

'Perhaps it would have been better if she had, then at least I would have been forced to realise what was happening,' he said grimly. 'But Cynthia, being Cynthia, just compensated by being busier than ever. After Dominic was born and she realised how untidy and disorganised motherhood actually was I think she was appalled. But it had been her idea to have a child and she could never bring herself to admit a mistake. She handed Dom over almost completely to a nanny, or should I say nannies. Cyn was never satisfied with one for long, perhaps she was trying to compensate for not being the loving mother she thought she should be by finding fault with the mother-substitutes she was providing. A kind of self-flagellation.

'Anyway, she never worried me with her domestic concerns—that wasn't part of the image. She just bottled them all up inside herself and I was too involved in building the business to notice anything. By the time Dom was two we had drifted so far apart that there was really nothing holding us together except the trappings of marriage. Quite frankly she bored me and her insistence on maintaining appearances seemed not only futile, it was condemning us to emotional stagnation. So I moved out, into an apartment, and simply never went back. I was already so uninvolved in Dom's life—I was away two weeks out of every four, and by the time I got home at night Dom was usually long asleep—that I doubt if he realised my absence. I knew that I would always support him financially, of course ...' he shrugged and on his face Gina saw the wry self-recrimination, 'but since I hadn't considered that I was ready for fatherhood anyway I was quite happy to leave him with Cyn and only visit occasionally. But that didn't work. Dom wouldn't go out anywhere with me, of course, and seeing him at home with Cyn was a disaster. She bitterly resented my shattering her carefully nurtured image of a perfect marriage. I guess I can't blame her for trying to turn him against me.'

'But it was cruel, if she used him as a pawn,' Gina began, not able to understand his lack of bitterness.

'No more cruel than I. Indifference can be a worse cruelty. And I *was* indifferent. I was enjoying the fruits of my success, plus a new kind of personal freedom after years in the straightjacket of boredom. So I can't turn around and accuse Cyn of setting my son against me when for years I didn't give a damn.'

'So why *have* you changed?' Gina probed cautiously, understanding better than he knew about the freedom to be oneself. 'Why is Dom with you now? Did your ... is Cynthia dead?'

'Good God, no!' He looked astonished that she could think so. 'She's still around, somewhere in the States at the moment, pursuing the perfect ideal still, I suppose.' That didn't sound like a man suffering the pangs of a thwarted love. 'No, I guess I just walked slap bang into the brick wall of responsibility and realised how much of a selfish bastard I had been. I didn't even know Nic was deaf, you see, until last year.'

Gina was truly appalled. 'You mean she didn't *tell* you?'

'She was petrified I would blame her, as if measles were something she invented.' His mouth pulled tight. 'But that's Cynthia all over, terrified of anything she can't control ... my temper as well as infectious diseases. I guess in building me up in Dom's mind to be some kind of monster she had convinced herself of it too. She didn't know herself for months anyway—she didn't spend that much time with him and the nannies had changed so frequently that the new one didn't know Dom's capabilities. She just thought he was naturally slow and particularly spoiled and wilful ... the last two are quite true regardless of his hearing, and he *does* respond to loud noises, or at least the vibrations from them, so to an inexperienced person it might seem that the problem was mental rather than physical. When the nanny finally did take him to the doctor he was diagnosed as potentially autistic. He was sent to a centre for assessment where they found out about his deafness.'

'Oh, Nic,' Gina said softly, feeling an ache in her breast. Her own horror story paled beside the young boy's. How bewildered he must have been, incapable of understanding what had happened to him or why and with no one, stable, familiar, loving planet in his small universe to hold on to. Gina, too, had had a mother in whom maternal instincts had not fully blossomed but at least she had had the company of her sisters and when dark fate had stalked her she had been old enough to fight back ... even though she too had gone through a trauma something like Nic's.

'To cut a long story short Cynthia struggled through on her own for another six months doing all the right things—hiring tutors, taking him to clinics, still playing the perfect mother who loved her son in spite of the fact that she really had no idea how to handle him. Her standards were too high and I think she knew that Dom would never meet them but she had to try. In the end she wrote to me and told me that she was considering putting Dom in a special residential school.'

'An *institution*!' Gina felt a wave of icy rage, yet she knew that she ought to be more understanding. There *were* parents who couldn't cope with their child's deafness, even normally loving parents. They felt too angry, or too guilty, or they just didn't have the patience or personal strength to perservere with what they saw as a futile struggle. Gina had met parents like that at the centre and pitied them as much as she pitied their child.

'It might have been best for him, if he hadn't had a father,' Leo said tautly, 'and Cynthia had no reason to believe that I would take him.'

'But you did.' Gina's eyes were shimmering pools of blackness.

'Don't put me on a pedestal, sweetheart, my reasons were less than pure,' he told her drily. 'Pride, at first, and a certain self-righteous satisfaction that Cynthia had fallen on her face. I thought I could handle it as simply and effectively as I handled everything else in my life. Dom soon put me straight. He was like a stone, never reacting, never responding. There was a maid, Fenny, of Cynthia's whom he had latched on to and I made the mistake of telling him I'd try and get her to come and look after him. She was leaving to get married and wouldn't, not for all the bribes I could offer—she knew Dom better than I, of course. Cyn hadn't let him go to school so I couldn't spring that on him as well as everything else. I hired Miss Hamilton who at least has his respect for her tenaciousness, if not his complete co-operation. She made me realise that Dom was never going to make any real progress unless he had the incentive to start communicating. For that he had to have someone with whom he *wanted* to communicate, someone who would share pride in his achievements in a very personal way, who wouldn't mix him up with the kind of conflict that Cyn had thrust upon him.'

'You mean he wanted to be loved,' murmured Gina.

'A self-evident truth, you might think, but it hadn't been to me. And when I realised that I realised something else . . . that I wanted to love him, wanted him to love *me*. It was more than blood or some abstract ideal of parenthood—the way Cyn had seen it.

I didn't give a damn that he wasn't perfect physically, I just wanted him to have a *chance*. What's in him is part of me. I can't give him his hearing back but I can be his ears for as long as he needs me to be. And I can give him *myself*. That's what we're doing here, on Paradise for the next few months. Finding out about each other. And so much happiness depends on it you can understand, can't you, why this time is so important to me? Why, at the moment, *you're* important? I couldn't make Fenny stay, but I *can* make you.'

'Why didn't you just explain all this before?'

'Because I had no reason to think it would make any difference,' he said, with devastating honesty. He moved his long body, relaxing the tension brought on by the reminiscence and his skin rippled like oiled silk. 'But you do care, don't you, about Nic?' His eyes narrowed on her vulnerable expression. 'Mind you, I wouldn't trust you around him if he were seventeen rather than seven, but I doubt that a woman of your experience would have much of a taste for young boys.'

It was like a slap in the face after the implied trust of the last fifteen minutes. Colour ran up under Gina's skin.

'You bastard,' she said shakily.

'For speaking the truth?' he said evenly.

'*Your* version of the truth,' Gina sat up, brushing the sand from her elbows and hands.

'Is there any other?'

'I didn't know he was married,' she rasped.

'Would it have mattered?' he asked cynically.

'Of course it would have!' She threw her hair back over her shoulders and gave him a look of furious haughtiness.

'Wasn't your sister Diane involved in a divorce suit last year?'

'Do you always judge a book by what's next to it on the shelf?' Gina flared.

'If it's by the same author,' he said smoothly.

'Well, I didn't know he was married,' she snapped. 'If I had I would never have——' she caught herself.

'Gone to bed with him?'

'I never——'

'Don't give me that, Virginia,' he suddenly lost his cynical cool. 'We both know you're a sexy little piece. And Niven never dated women who didn't put out for him . . . though up until you came along he had had the decency to be discreet about it. Your technique must have been mind-blowing if it was enough to make Niven forget which side his bread was buttered on.'

'You know nothing about it,' she said hoarsely but he interrupted her with a few muttered words of Fijian. Heat streaked along her veins as she realised where she had heard him use them before.

'Did you think that just because I haven't said anything I didn't realise it was you?' he growled at her and Gina flinched at the scorching look he gave her. 'I knew as soon as I saw those scars, the day after the storm. But you knew all along that it was me . . . so don't try and sell me on your celibacy.' She went white at the taunt, and clenched her teeth tightly to hold back pain. 'You have some pretty powerful urges pulsing in that sweet-looking body of yours and I don't expect that you were ever taught much about self-control.'

Gina exploded to her feet, pale and shaking with the effort of finding the words that had been so long denied her. Her fury was like a thick rope around her neck but she struggled against its tightening bond. She hated him then as she had never hated anyone, even Niven . . . for being whole-bodied without flaws or scars to mar his male beauty, for being so tenderly ruthless with Nic and yet so utterly, brutally vicious with her.

'No, I wasn't taught anything, but I learned. Oh, how I learned!' she spat at him in a powerful, rasping whisper that tore out of her mouth with tormented speed. She stood tautly over him, quivering like a bow-string, launching the ice-tipped arrows of bitterness point-blank into his upturned face. That they struck their mark gave her no satisfaction, for as his face stiffened into a grey mask she saw his anger give way to a shocked pity that turned her agonised words back on herself and made her only hate him the more.

'You think *you* know more about self-control than I do? *No one* knows more than I do. I'll tell you what it is! Self-control is being sixteen, with the world and everything in it set out before you ... and not being able to reach out and touch it. It's having your voice ripped out of your throat by a moment's carelessness and having to lie in some dreary hospital bed and listen to people tell you how *lucky* you are.' The word was thick with loathing. 'How *lucky* you are to have only lost your voice, how *lucky* you are to be alive and after every new operation how maybe, next time ...' She gave a laugh that was hoarse and bitter. 'Self-control is four years, *four years*, walled up inside yourself ... not being able to argue, or explain, or defend yourself; always being talked *at* or *over* instead of *to*; pretending that you don't notice that your own family is embarrassed by you; pretending not to care that suddenly no one bothers to pass the time of day with you, or treats you like a freak or a mental defective. Self-control is learning to cope with not being able to cry when you need to, or laugh when you're happy, or sing along to your favourite tune on the radio.'

Her voice broke but she drove herself on, lashing herself with the memory of the pain, the loneliness, the emptiness that she had been trying so desperately to put behind her.

'Self-control is the mask you put on so everyone thinks you're OK when really you're dying inside. It's what you use when you find out that the one person in the *world* you thought really understood you, and accepted you, really doesn't give a damn. That not only doesn't he love you, he's *repulsed* by you. Not only has he a wife, but a mistress too, a rich mistress with a voice

like silk whom he wants to marry, only he can't risk
involving her in a divorce or scandal because of some
morals clause in her dead husband's will. So they found
someone stupid enough, pathetic enough to actually
imagine a normal man might fall in love with a dumb
girl. And they didn't need to worry that I'd blab the
truth at the vital moment, did they? Oh, no, what luck
that I happened to cross Niven's path just at the right
time. See how *lucky* I always am?'

Tears were streaming down her face so that she could
hardly see the man who had risen unsteadily to his feet
through the hot blur. She didn't want to see him
anyway. What had made her think, even for a moment,
that he might be different? That he might be capable of
seeing her as she was, not through the distorting
mirrors that others had held up to her?

'They used me, you use me, Nic uses me!' she cried,
with the last of her vocal strength. 'Everybody wants
something from me but nobody ever gives anything to
me!'

On that cry from the heart of the sixteen-year-old
who had too quickly matured but never quite given up
the childish fantasy of one day being loved, cherished
and protected for herself alone, Gina fled.

The outstretched golden arm failed to stop her and
when the man's powerful body sprang into motion he
stumbled over the small forgotten figure who had long
abandoned his sulks for the fascination of an
incomprehensible battle.

Oh, God, Nic, what have I done? He saw the words
form on his . . . on the *man's* lips, and was rooted to the
spot, not by the strong hands now gripping him, but by
the strange vibrations he was picking up, and the
tormented expression on the adult face.

Gina was crying and he should be angry, but why
was the man holding him looking so ill? The yellow eyes
weren't hard and horrid, they looked all shimmery like
the flat golden sand on a hot day. Nic's heart thumped

in his chest, making him feel sick. The shimmery eyes made him feel frightened, but not in the usual way he felt frightened. *He* wasn't supposed to look like that, all terrible and sad. What did it mean? He was torn between the urge to run after Gina and a strong desire to stay and watch the man to see what he would do next. Maybe he would say something. He was always talking to Nic, explaining things, even when Nic didn't want to know. But maybe, just this time, he would listen.

CHAPTER SEVEN

GINA stripped off her pareu and the sand-encrusted cameo and stood under a shower as hot as she could take it, closing her eyes as the water poured over her face, rinsing away sand and tears. She was dimly aware of having passed Pamela Smythe in the hallway, and her startled exclamation. The other woman had not seemed to resent being relieved of her job; in fact she had confided to Gina that she was glad to be rid of the 'little demon' and spent most of the time sunbathing or reading in her room while she waited for transport off the island. 'Don't bother setting your sights on the boss,' she had warned Gina, 'he doesn't play around with the hired help. I gave it my best shot but he never even nibbled.' Gina didn't think she could face those curious green eyes over lunch. She didn't think she could face lunch at all.

After her shower she still felt battered and bruised, and utterly exhausted from her outburst of self-pitying rage. Yet it had released some of the pressure that she had felt after years of holding her feelings in and the exhaustion was oddly welcome.

Gina fastened the shutters on her window, closing out the invading sun, and fell into the soft bed, pulling up the crisp white cotton sheet over her nakedness. She lay on her back staring up at the big, twin-bladed fan that spun slowly, hypnotically, above her ...

She woke disorientated, puzzled by the darkness, then she turned her head and saw a vague shape on the other side of the room. The shape moved, loomed, and the light beside the bed clicked on, dazzling her.

'How are you feeling?' the voice rumbled softly,

golden eyes assessing her sleep-dazed features.

'I . . . what's the time?' Her first instinct was to sit up, but she remembered her nakedness, her bare throat, and pulled the sheet defensively to her chin.

'Nearly eight,' he told her, sitting down on the edge of the bed so that the sheet pulled taut across her body.

'W . . . what are you doing here?' she mumbled, blinking the stickiness of sleep out of her darkly apprehensive eyes.

'You slept through lunch and it looked like you were going to sleep through dinner. Liana didn't know whether to wake you or not. I said I'd come and see.'

'Well, now you've seen, and I'm awake,' said Gina, unnerved by the strange, solemn expression on his face. 'If you leave I'll get up and get dressed for dinner.'

'I think we should talk first, don't you?' he said, with such quiet purposefulness that Gina's stomach began to churn. She felt far too vulnerable trapped in the bed with him sitting there, elegantly attired in a white silk shirt and dark trousers while she only had the cotton sheet.

'Can't it wait?' she said pettishly. 'I'm hungry.'

'Dinner's not ready yet,' he told her calmly, shifting so that he was leaning towards her, placing one hand on the far side of her body so that a bridge of silk-wrapped muscle was formed over her breasts. 'And, no, it can't wait.'

'Where's Nic?' she husked, dipping her chin further beneath the sheet.

'In bed, asleep.'

'But I usually——'

'He came in here and gave *you* a kiss,' said Leo, telling her that he knew what she usually did. 'It was a rather rough one too, he was disappointed that you didn't wake up. I explained that crying had made you very, very tired.'

'And I suppose you also explained why I was crying in the first place,' she snapped hoarsely.

His gaze was unflinching. 'I said that until you get to know someone you can hurt them in all kinds of ways without realising it. I told him I was angry, and my anger made me say things that weren't true. I told him that one of the reasons I was angry was because I knew that I had been wrong about you but I was too full of stubborn pride to admit it.'

'Very clever,' said Gina bitterly, thinking that he was capable of turning any situation to his advantage.

'And very honest,' the broad-boned cheeks hollowed wryly. 'You rather left us in the lurch back there and miraculously he seemed to expect something from me. I gave him the truth. It was all I could think of on the spur of the moment. I'm sorry if I hurt you.'

Gina closed her eyes, feeling the sting in her sinuses. Leo Sterne looking abashed and tender frightened her even more than Leo the lion.

'Gina? I never did get to ask my questions down there on the beach.' She felt his hand on her hair, tangled across the pillow, and her eyes flew open, black with resentment.

'Oh, I thought you had all the answers.'

He shook his head, eyes clear as amber. 'I wasn't going to ask about Niven, remember? But my temper got the better of me. I was going to ask about this.' She flinched as his hand moved from her hair to draw a line across the white sheet where it guarded her throat.

'No——' she whispered. Hadn't she told him enough?

'Yes. I know I've been a bastard but you can't throw things at me like that without explaining. Don't you think I deserve a chance to make amends? Or is playing the martyr something that you enjoy?'

She flared at that last taunt, with its tiny grain of truth. It *had* been satisfying to possess the secret knowledge that he was wrong about her. Like Nic she had withheld information as a form of control.

'Are you going to crucify me for being human enough to have weaknesses? The evidence *was* damning against you, Gina. Won't you help me understand what makes you so different from the person I thought you to be?' he went on and the flare of anger was swamped by weakness. He looked as if he would keep her there forever, until she told him. 'What happened when you were sixteen?'

So she told him, huskily, each word following the last without thought or direction. She told him with her voice and the fleeting expressions that crossed her softly illuminated face and what she told him curled the fingers that rested against the far side of her body into a white-knuckled fist. The husky voice sometimes sank to a whisper as she spoke of the despair, the struggle, the alienation and the slow battle against ignorance and indifference. She didn't talk about her family but the shrewd golden eyes read the truth from the omission, heard the ache of loneliness in the damaged voice, the loss and bewilderment.

'And this last operation ... *is* it the last?' he asked tautly when she stumbled out of words, approaching the time she had met Niven.

She nodded, eyes still filled with memories. 'Except ... I'll be having some plastic surgery done at the end of the year. They ... the doctor didn't do any before because of all the surgery I was having—there didn't seem to be any point when another operation might be just around the corner.'

'Will it get rid of all the scarring?' he probed cruelly, watching her flinch.

'Not all. Most,' said Gina tightly. It was just as she had thought. He also found them repelling.

'Have you always been so self-conscious about them?'

'Wouldn't you be?' asked Gina bitterly.

'To a certain extent. But you seem to be almost

obsessive. Don't you know that all those nervous little mannerisms of yours—ducking your chin, fingering that ribbon you wear—just draw attention to what you're trying to hide?' He paused and Gina stiffened, reading the determination in the tight lines of his face. 'Was it Niven who made you so afraid of being yourself? All those months and years of suffering must have made you maturer than most girls your age. Why couldn't you dismiss Niven as the two-timing bastard he was instead of letting it eat at you as it obviously has?'

'You said you wouldn't ask me about Niven,' she said desperately.

'But you need to talk about him. You haven't got all the poison out of your system yet. Spit it out, Gina. Tell *me*. He hurt me and mine too, remember.'

She turned her head to one side but his strong hand turned it back and stayed, hard and warm, on her jaw.

'Did you love him?'

She shuddered as she remembered the pathetic mock-romance that had ensnared her feelings. Her own wretched gullibility rose to haunt her as she remembered the stranger revealed to her in that dreadful bedroom after she had finally emerged to pull on her clothes. Niven had first tried to appeal to her understanding.

'I had to do it, Gina, please ... let me explain. Our marriage has been over for ages but Kathy wouldn't give me a divorce and that brother of hers makes sure that whatever Kathy wants she gets ... he'd have ruined me if I tried to go against him. I had to tell him who you were ...' so those were the murmurs she had heard while locked in the icy bathroom '... but don't worry, he'll make sure it's all very, very discreet.'

When he saw that it wasn't working he had tried a different tack. 'I didn't know he was going to turn up, honestly, Gina. I knew Kathy was coming back early from the States but I never imagined that he would be with her, really.' Gina would never believe anything he said again. She walked to the bedroom door, with Niven following. He took the stairs two at a time and stopped her near the bottom.

'I just wanted her to stop being a millstone around my neck. I met this woman, you see . . .' Gina flinched, her eyes stony. 'I've been seeing her for a while. We want to get married. But under the terms of her husband's will she forfeits everything if she breaks some stupid morality clause. It was getting too hard to keep things quiet and I *had* to make sure that she wasn't mentioned if Kathy agreed to a divorce. Don't you see, all the money I have is Kathy's. Trina and I need her inheritance . . .' he had trailed off at the jerk of Gina's dark head. She had not even been betrayed for *love*. For passion maybe, for money, but not for any genuine depth of emotion, such as *she* had felt.

And then Niven had said the final words, the ones that had been so shattering.

'Don't look at me like that, Gina, I didn't make you any promises, did I? Hell, you don't even really love me, it's just gratitude. You should stop being so intense about everything. Maybe if you showed you were willing there'd be plenty of guys willing to overlook your physical defects. Some guys are even turned on by people like you.'

People like you. Freaks. The pain had been incredible.

'Gina? *Gina*!' She opened her eyes, unaware that she had even been speaking, feeling the hands heavy on her shoulders and seeing Leo Sterne's face only a breath away from hers filled with a smouldering fury. 'He said *that* to you, after what the bastard had done? My God, I should have pulped him while I had the chance.'

Gina trembled before the violence that seethed in the powerful body. 'For telling the truth?'

'Truth?' he was incredulous. 'For implying that no

normal man would want to make love to you? And you *believed* that?'

'*He* didn't,' Gina cried huskily.

'I wouldn't call Niven exactly normal myself. The man is a pathological creep——' he stopped, the hands on her shoulders clenching, his head jerking back. 'What in the hell do you mean he didn't?'

Gina hid her eyes beneath dark lashes. 'I mean he never made love to me. It was the first time I had been to his place. He got me drunk and put me into bed, that's all.' Her smile was a small, bitter one. 'It certainly wasn't because I wasn't willing. *He* was always the one to draw back, and I thought it was only because he wanted to protect my innocence until we got engaged.'

There was a stifled sound above her head. 'Innocence . . . you mean . . . there's been no one?'

'Don't sound so surprised,' said Gina, still not looking at him. 'I'd only just turned sixteen when it happened. Strange as it may sound I hadn't really been interested in boys up until then. I was only just beginning to——'

'Imitate your elder sisters,' he said drily, causing her glance to fly upwards. He captured it easily and held it with golden confidence. 'So that's why you're such a strange mixture. Mature in some ways but not in others. You missed out all those growing, experimenting years. Surely there must have been some boys . . .'

Gina swallowed. 'Only the ones my mother press-ganged into it. They didn't know how to treat me and I hated being embarrassed by their awkwardness. I couldn't flirt or flatter. I couldn't joke or gossip. I was dumb. A bore.'

'Silent, perhaps, but never dumb.' His hand stilled her bitter words, stroking the soft lips with his thumb. 'If they were so shallow perhaps you were better off without them.'

With hindsight Gina knew it to be true. It was that isolation from people that had forced her to think and act for herself, free of peer pressure. It had pulled her back from the brink of the genetic trap. She could never, now, live the kind of frivolous, self-seeking life her mother and sisters did. She had watched it from the sidelines for too long not to be able to realise the inner vaccum that was masked by all the frenetic socialising.

'So Niven was the first man who paused to entice the innocent baby kitten out from the safety of her cosy corner. No wonder you fell hard. I could almost wish, though, that he had taken you properly to his bed.'

Gina reacted wildly, trying to throw off his restraining hands, eyes glittering at his callousness as she tried to work her hands free of the sheet that he held tightly across her shoulders. 'You think I'd feel better about it now, if he had?' she flung at him furiously when he refused to be dislodged by her struggles.

'From a strictly logical point of view, yes,' he stunned her by saying, and continuing relentlessly, 'because I think that he's succeeded in thoroughly confusing you. I don't think that you're the kind of woman who could love without wanting to make love. There's a lot of passion in you, it shows up in your drawings, the way they almost seem to strain at the limitations of line and dimension ... it shows in your compassionate attitude to Dom and your strong emotions. So now you feel a fool for falling in love with Niven, but you can't stop remembering that you wanted him. He was responsible for your sexual awakening, yet he wasn't sexually attracted to you. That shames you, and somehow you've twisted it up in your mind that it was because of those scars he rejected you ... perhaps because it's easier for your pride to accept than the fact that he was probably sleeping with this other woman ... presumably the one he married.'

'Thank you for that piece of amateur psychology,' Gina said, on the verge of fresh tears but refusing to let them fall, her eyes dark pools of pain.

'I'm just telling you what my instincts tell me. Don't

feel ashamed of your physical needs, Gina. Niven was good-looking and very adept at manipulating women. Kathy knew what he was like all along but she still clung to the hope that he would change. She always took him back ... but that final flaunting made her realise that she was wasting her life on a worthless fool. You see, Niven isn't capable of any great depth of emotion. True passion involves sexual love, not just sex. I think you'll find, as you begin to explore your own sexuality, that you need a partner who is capable of your own kind of passion. If you *had* slept with Niven you would have found out for yourself that he wasn't the kind of man who could satisfy your emotional or physical needs, and perhaps the feeling of betrayal wouldn't have been quite so great, or so lasting.'

'I suppose next you'll be telling me that I didn't really love him,' she rejected, her body heating with all this talk of sex. 'You're going to tell me Niven was right, it was just gratitude.'

'And sex,' he watched her blush with a glint of satisfaction, the sensually narrow lip curving at the corners as he awaited her reaction.

'I loved him,' she hissed fiercely.

'Is it so beyond the realms of possibility that perhaps you confused your first sexual stirrings with love?'

'Yes. If I hadn't loved him I wouldn't have felt the way I did.'

The even eyebrows shot up as he pursued her. 'You mean he wouldn't have been able to make you want him.'

'I ...' she faltered and rallied. If she admitted any doubt that would make her no better than Diane or Eileen, who gave their favours to anyone who took their momentary fancy. 'That's exactly what I mean!'

'No?'

There was a tiny, singing silence as Gina realised the challenge that she had unknowingly issued.

'No,' she breathed as he smiled into her eyes.

'You're not afraid of me, are you, Gina? I've said I'm sorry for hurting you, and I promise I won't hurt you again. Besides, once I see those scars you'll be safe, won't you? Because you don't believe any man could look at them and still find you attractive.'

Realising what he was going to do Gina tried to hold the sheet tighter but he pulled it away easily, his hands coming up to crush hers and hold them away from what she would hide.

'Don't——' Gina whispered, hating him for his insensitivity.

Still holding her hands his eyes went over her vulnerable throat in a clinical study. She shrank within herself without moving a muscle. He had promised he wouldn't hurt her but now he was going to . . . badly.

'Not pretty,' he conceded at agonising length. 'But not hideous either. A shock at first sight, and most people wouldn't be able to hide that shock, but afterwards . . .' his eyes wandered down over the hills and valleys of the white sheet. 'They're only a small part of you, Gina. One small, physical flaw.' His voice deepened to a husky drawl as he looked at her frozen face with its dark halo. 'Haven't you ever heard of that Middle Eastern philosophy about perfection . . . that nothing of beauty should be utterly perfect lest it attract the wrath of God. They even *created* deliberate flaws in beautiful objects, which only served to emphasise the beauty that surrounded them. I tried to live with perfection, Gina, and couldn't. Striving for it can break you.'

Gina couldn't break free from the compelling magic of his eyes, even when she felt the warmth of his hand move to her throat and his fingers begin to trace the network of scars.

'Don't let these make you ashamed of your body, or of your natural instincts.'

He bent his head and Gina made a soft, choking sound as she felt the touch of his mouth where his hand had been. Her freed fingers curled into a small fist beside her head as she experienced the first, gentle, non-medical touches on her throat for years. Having him kissing the scars that she had hated so long was shocking, almost indecent, and she felt disturbing sensations erupting up and down her stiffened body, not daring to move. His mane brushed her chin, his torso hovering over her, radiating heat and a clean, soapy scent that seemed to go to her head like the bouquet of some intoxicating vintage.

'Does it look as though I find them repulsively awful?' he muttered against her throat. 'Does it feel as if I can't bear to touch them?' Now she felt his tongue, warm and moist and slightly rough, lapping at her as if he would drink up her pain and she fought against the feelings welling against the restraints of reason.

'Leo——' He smothered the beginning of her protest with his mouth, a very skilful mouth with a tongue that stroked and darted and made it seem as if she had just bitten into some exotic, erotic fruit of explosive sweetness.

Her hands were quite free now but she lost track of his until she felt the sheet peeled away to settle across the jutting bones of her hip. She cried out and put her hands up to push him away and felt the silk of his shirt cling to the heat of her fingers, felt the ripple of muscle as he drew back until she could see his face. She panicked at the look in his narrowed eyes, a kind of predatory hunger that looked dangerously uncontrolled and yet, when he soothed her, his voice was soft, and gentle and reassuringly controlled, although what he said should have frightened her more.

'I said I wouldn't hurt you, and I won't. All I'm going to do is pet you a little ... touch you, admire you, make you feel good, show you some of the woman-pleasure that is ahead of you.'

His smile was full of mysterious promises and Gina felt heavy with a lethargy that pinned her to the bed. He wasn't touching her and yet it was as though he was already pressing down on top of her, holding her down with his maleness, and his words prickled an awareness over her exposed skin that made her gasp. She tried to control her shallow breathing so that her breasts didn't rise and fall quite so boldly but her tiny gasps delighted him and the golden eyes watched her body's involuntary response and began to burn. A low sound of satisfaction came from the sensuous line of his mouth.

'Unbutton my shirt,' he purred to her but she lay, unmoving, looking at him with a dark, shocked, wide-eyed innocence that was as disarming as it was arousing. He tore open his shirt and pulled her stiff and wary hands against the muscular chest, arching slightly with satisfaction at the way her nails curved lightly into his skin.

'Yes, touch me, Gina, the way I'm going to touch you.'

The sight of her hands against his bare flesh made her fall deeper under his masculine spell. The dark golden curls felt soft and springy under her fingers. Niven's chest had been hairless and he had never seemed to get any pleasure from her touching him. Gina was stunned at the way this powerful lion of a man tautened at each small flex of her fingers, his eyes closing, his lips parting, cheeks hollowing as he sucked in his breath. His eyelids lifted slowly and he smiled lazily at the expression on her face.

'Now it's my turn.'

His hand moved and they both watched as his long, brown fingers drifted across her golden flesh, down to where it turned creamy-white.

'I like this,' he whispered softly as her own fingers clenched tightly in the soft whorls of hair as the world rocked violently around her. 'I like it that you don't sunbathe nude, that you keep your body private for me.'

His fingers curved, cupped, his thumb dragging slowly across the pink crests until Gina moaned, feeling her breasts harden in his hand until they felt tight and hot, the nipples aching badly. Sometimes she had felt like this when Niven touched her through her clothing and she hadn't liked being left with the wound-up, painful tenseness when he drew the line, as he always did, at anything more.

She braced herself now against the hollow sensation that was going to follow when suddenly the gentle, feathering movements became firmer ... a delicious kneading followed by a tugging pull that startled her out of her sensuous lethargy.

'Don't——'

'Why not, I think you like me touching your breasts ... they're very sensitive ...' he murmured, his other hand joining in the fondling, gliding silkily, stroking, stoking the fires he had lit along her skin as he told her how delightful he found her body. The words which at any other time she would have found crude and offensive only excited her more and she gave a soft sigh which made him laugh, equally softly, and touch her again.

'Like that?' he asked huskily. 'Would you like to feel my mouth there, too?'

He bent his head without waiting for an answer and she nearly screamed at the incredible sensation of his lips and tongue appeasing the ache, making soft, contented suckling sounds as he enjoyed her arousal. Her hands slid over his shoulders under his shirt, to grip the hard shoulder blades, her head sinking back into the pillow as her spine arched off the sheets.

'Oh, Leo...' she squirmed as she felt his hand leave her swollen breast to splay out over her stomach, the tips of his fingers curving under the edge of the sheet to press down on the hard ridge of bone that was cushioned by the soft mound of flesh and the first, shy curls of midnight hair. Before Gina could register the firm pressure that suddenly drew all sensation downwards his hand had moved again, this time to brush lightly against her inner thighs and Gina shuddered, opening her mouth to plead, to tell him what she wanted . . .

Her lips moved but nothing came out, not even a whisper. She sucked in a huge breath and struggled against the nightmare that disrupted the beautiful dream of passion but could only manage one, tortured word.

'Leo!' She pushed frantically against him and he must have felt the surge of fear that superceded passion for he lifted his head, prepared to soothe once more. She saw the blind-eyed look he gave her and opened her mouth again, her head going from side to side in despair as she felt the hard ball in her throat. He shook his head sharply and she saw the golden eyes come back into focus.

'What's the matter, am I hurting you?'

Her mouth worked helplessly and she almost burst with the frustration.

'You can't talk? Are you in pain? Does this happen sometimes?'

She mimed and he caught on quickly, stopping the panicky fluttering of her hands in gentle capture.

'When you're upset? Emotional? Excited?' he guessed and suddenly the worried frown was placed by a grin. 'Have I made you speechless with violent delight?'

Gina froze with horror, realising that was exactly what he had done. He hadn't only seduced away her voice, the very breath from her body, but also every ounce of common sense. She closed her mouth with a snap and yanked up the sheet to cover the blush that was settling over her entire body.

'Angry at me?' he mocked gently. 'For showing you that perhaps it was not your heart that Niven shattered but your pride and self-confidence? I bet you never even let him see your scars, you never trusted him enough. If it was love, it was the puppy love that you were long overdue for. You're angry at being taken for a fool but all of us make fools of ourselves at one time or another about love and sex.'

Gina sat upright, wrapping the sheet around her, glaring at him, almost glad that she couldn't speak, for what would she say? Although she had been willing for Niven to love her body she *had* held back an important part of herself, without which it would have been impossible for them to have a true understanding of each other. She hadn't known Niven at all, and he had made no real effort to know her. She had hidden from him her doubts, her fears, and had been grateful to him for not pressuring her into painful self-examination. Yet if he had really cared, he would have.

She closed her eyes and took three or four deep breaths, feeling the ache in her throat ease.

'You needn't think——' she began in a raspy voice, desperate to convince him that what had just happened must never happen again, 'that this means ... means ...'

'It means that you're a woman and I'm a man and we're attracted to each other,' he said with a lazy-eyed simplicity that reduced everything to basics. He began to re-button his shirt as he talked calmly over her confusion. 'I certainly don't feel embarrassed about finding you desirable and I don't see why you should look as though you expect me to shrink away from you because you enjoyed a little friendly love-play.'

'You mean you don't think I'm a tramp when I respond to you, only when I respond to other men,' she managed in a guttural mutter.

He gave a patient sigh. 'Gina, a woman is only a tramp when she doesn't respect herself, when she uses her body as a kind of commodity to buy instant self-gratification without taking the time to explore the deeper dimensions of a relationship. I've had women as lovers who weren't in love with me, who had had previous lovers, who were frank and open about their sexuality. They weren't tramps. They were caring, giving women who were at ease with themselves and weren't afraid of showing their feelings. And they expected more from a man than a night's entertainment ... friendship, companionship, respect ... without those the sex act is just that, an act.'

'What was that just now, an audition?' Gina lifted her chin proudly, forgetting about the scars. Somehow they didn't matter with a man who had kissed and stroked them. She was highly suspicious about all this talk about caring and giving women. Did he expect her to be one?

'Only if you want it to be,' he said, rising from the bed and looking down at her with a glint in his eyes that made her unsure of whether he was teasing her or gently putting her of. He tucked his shirt into his trousers and changed the subject suddenly. 'My plane will be back tomorrow. Miss Smythe is leaving on it. Will you stay on ... for another week or two ... until Nic is more confident with me?'

'You called him Nic.' she said faintly, trying to readjust to the prosaic.

'It's all he seems to answer to these days,' he said drily, without visible rancour. 'Will you stay? If you have a deadline on those illustrations Miss Smythe can deliver them for you; she owes me *some* kind of service for the exorbitant fee I paid for her ineptitude. Is there any reason why you need to go back to Auckland straight away?'

'You ... you'll let me go tomorrow, if I want to?' she asked warily. 'No blackmail, no threats?'

'No tantrums,' he added gravely. 'Yes, I'll let you go. But I'd rather you didn't. You can work here if you have to. I'll even pose for you, if you need a model.'

Her pulse-rate lifted at his dead-pan expression. Why did she immediately think of him as a nude? Damn it, what was he doing to her? One minute he was looking at her as if she was a desirable woman, the next he was teasing her as if she was a blushing schoolgirl.

The tiny resonant echoes of pleasure that still shivered from cell to cell in her body tempted her to say yes. Is that why he had started to make love to her? As another method of persuasion when he realised that he could no longer use more forcible means of coercion?

'I want to go!' she declared, squaring her shoulders, rejecting the comfort of lies. Once she had allowed misty fantasies to obscure her reason and look where it had led.

'And Nic?' he asked quietly, his head turned from the light into shadow, so that she could only see the clean smooth line of jaw. He had shaved before coming to her room and his cheek against her skin had been like the caress of velvet.

'Nic will understand. He knows I work,' she said stiffly.

'Ah, Gina, at least be honest.' His voice was like velvet, too. 'You're not running *to* something, you're running away from it. Don't make *me* responsible for Niven's crimes, don't attribute his motives to me. We're nothing alike. I don't abuse trust. And once I do decide to take on a responsibility I carry it through. I want you to stay, yes. But not only for Nic. For me. And for you. I find myself wondering what it would be like to be your first lover.' He leaned forward and brushed her furrowed forehead with his lips. 'And I think that now you're wondering too.'

CHAPTER EIGHT

GINA watched the Lear jet swoop into the sky with sudden dismay. She should have gone. She should be up there, sitting next to Pamela Smythe, looking forward to getting back to real life again instead of standing here, waving at the diminishing speck of common sense. She could feel Leo's eyes on her but she refused to look at him. She had probably just made the biggest mistake of her life and she wasn't sure how it had happened. Right up until breakfast, through the whole, long, restless night, she had been determined that she was going to leave. She was going to be sensible. She wasn't going to take any more chances. And yet here she was, ensnared again by the magician's spell.

A small hand tightened in her grasp and she smiled down at Nic who was pleased at having vanquished his opponent. He had been allowed to get into the cockpit and look around the controls before take-off and had discovered with ill-concealed awe that his father knew what everything was and what it did. That his father could *fly*.

They began walking back to the villa, Gina signing and talking to the little boy, pretending to ignore the man sauntering along beside them with a quiet triumph of his own. At dinner the previous night he had been charmingly bland yet Gina had felt more threatened than ever. She had gone straight back to her room afterwards and packed her few salvageable possessions into a borrowed suitcase. The situation had danger stamped all over it. Maybe Leo Sterne was capable of playing love games without getting burned but Gina wasn't. She had already fallen in love once with the wrong man and if Leo were right with his amateur analysis—that her love had arisen from her need to reconcile her physical feelings with her romantic expectations—then having an affair with him was the last thing she should do.

She grew hot at the thought of what had happened between them last night, but strangely she felt no shame. Leo had made it seem so natural ... and that was the trap. He was handsome, experienced, skilled at seduction and if she indicated she was willing he would hold nothing back in a physical relationship. By his own admission he had plenty of lovers, women who weren't scarred physically and emotionally, so what did he really want with Gina? Was it because of the lack of anyone else available? He was obviously a man with strong sex drives—was the enforced celibacy of his stay on Paradise chafing? He was willing to put up with it for Nic's sake, but if the opportunity presented itself no doubt he felt obliged to take it.

And yet he had restrained himself for her sake. He had been sincerely sorry for hurting her, had been so very gentle at first, then angry on her behalf. He could easily have continued making love to her, breaking down her barriers, ignoring her panic, and it wouldn't have been rape in the final analysis. Instead he had given her a choice, even though she didn't dare take the road he wanted her to choose.

In spite of her decision, Gina fell asleep with a smile curving her lips as she remembered his reassurances about her attractiveness as a woman. He needn't have taken the risk of forcing her back into her shell by talking about her scars. He could have smoothly overlooked them, as most people did, as Niven had, and still aroused her with his skill. No, what he said, he believed, and that had enabled her to believe it, too.

She had been bounced awake the next morning by Nic, full of the news of the awful Miss Smythe's departure. *She wasn't any fun*, he signed, opening his eyes wide in a delighted exclamation point, *now we can have fun!*

Gina smiled at him, guiltily aware of the packed suitcase under her bed. Should she tell him gently, or firmly? Either way he was going to be hurt. He knew she was going to leave one day, but for Nic that 'one day' was some misty day in the future.

She had followed him reluctantly to the dining-room for breakfast, putting off the moment when she would have to dampen his high spirits. Leo wasn't there but Aileen greeted Nic with the news that after he had eaten he could join his father and the pilot on the airstrip. As a result Nic bolted his food and was gone before Gina had finished her fruit juice, taking her chance of breaking the news gently to him.

'Thank God I'm only going as far as Nandi in that thing,' Pamela Smythe groaned, taking an air-sickness pill with her coffee. 'I can't stand small planes. Give me a jumbo any day.'

'What will you be doing when you go back?' Gina asked politely, not really interested but trying to get rid of the churning sensation in her stomach that had nothing to do with the prospect of air-sickness. Should she go, could she stay? How could she leave without giving Nic a few days to adjust to the idea? Damn Leo for leaving it until the last minute to tell her about the plane. Had he done it deliberately?

She blinked, to find that Pamela had given her reply and left the table without her being aware of it.

'Mr Sterne said you might be going with her,' Aileen said, spreading marmalade on her toast, her sensible face giving nothing away.

'I . . . er . . . I haven't decided,' Gina lied, realising it wasn't a lie after all.

'It would be a pity if you did, just when Nic is settling down so well. A few more days and he might be secure enough to extend lessons. Another fortnight and I'll be off to Suva to get this cast removed. Then Nic and I can really get down to business.'

'Did L— did Mr Sterne ... say anything to you?' Gina asked suspiciously and received a twinkling look that made her feel as transparent as glass.

'Why, no, just that he had invited you to stay on longer, and that he hoped you would.'

'I expect he's grateful for my helping with Nic,' Gina said hurriedly.

'I expect he is,' Aileen agreed gravely and smiled to herself as the young woman excused herself from the table and scampered out of the dining-room.

Gina was still dithering in her room when Leo came to the half-open door.

'They're ready to go.' He saw the case by the bed and his jaw tightened as he gave her a crooked smile. 'I see you've made your decision.'

Gina found herself twisting her fingers in front of her as she stared at him. There was a slight slackness around his eyes, as if he hadn't slept very well either, and in their golden depths a genuine regret that rooted her to the spot. He looked sad yet cynical, as if he was resigned to disappointment, which was ridiculous. Anyone less likely to take defeat complacently Gina had yet to meet. She ran a hand nervously through her black tumble of curls, and touched her throat. The regret in the lion's eyes vanished, as they zeroed in on the teeth nibbling at her lip.

'If you need a bit longer to think about it, the plane will be back at the end of the week, with mail and supplies. Would you rather wait until then?'

'Why didn't you tell me that last night?' Gina asked in husky exasperation.

He shrugged, wary-eyed. 'I thought you might like the break quick and clean.'

'I ... if I did stay on for the rest of the week ... I ... you ...'

'Been skimping on your exercises, Gina?' His mouth twitched in the semblance of a smile. 'If you're trying to say that you'd like to stay but you're afraid I'll turn into a raging sex maniac the minute the plane takes off, relax. There's no obligation. All you ever have to do is say *no*. I think you're capable of doing that, aren't you?'

His teasing lightness was reassuring, allowing Gina to feel that the decision that she must leave could be safely put off for a little bit longer. Long enough to get Nic used to the idea, but not long enough for Leo to persuade her to do anything stupid.

She carried the *no* everywhere with her over the next few days, but was never given the chance to say it, because Leo never posed the question. The busy days were spent teaching Gina to snorkle, to surf-sail, to paddle an out-rigger . . . with Nic absorbing it all by osmosis. It was a time of delicate discovery for all three of them and Gina found herself enjoying the reprieve. She wasn't even aware of the relaxing of her own defensive attitude, the subtle differences in her responses to the lazy, unthreatening male, the way she blossomed under his gentle teasing. It was a long time since Gina had had such simple fun and she felt half-intoxicated by the liberating sound of her own laughter, her voice.

'My God, I think you're turning into a chatterer,' Leo said with mock disgust as they ate a picnic lunch on the sands. 'Aren't you in danger of running over your time limit?' He checked his watch. He and Nic had begun the tentative beginnings of a game when she had mentioned that the doctor had given her a rough guideline as to how much she should use her new voice each day. As if on cue the alarm on the digital monstrosity began to beep and he grinned at Nic and pointed. The little boy scrambled sandily over and pressed a finger against the face. He nodded at the feel of the tiny vibration.

'Shut-up time, Gina,' he shouted and giggled.

'Yes, shut up, Gina.' Leo poured himself a second glass of wine and raised it mockingly in salute. 'And to think I thought you were a nice, quiet girl.'

She gave him a little-girl look. 'And to think I

thought you were a rude, bad-tempered, overbearing tyrant.'

He drank, and topped her with a purring, 'Not to mention my being wild and wondrous and full of magic. Have you fallen under my spell yet, gypsy girl?'

She blushed and he laughed and Nic sat on his heels looking from one to the other and smiling, not knowing what was funny but not caring, as long as the happiness surrounded him like a charmed circle.

As well as teasing Leo liked to touch, holding her hand as they scrambled over rocks, guiding her down to the coral kingdom under the blue crystal surface of the lagoon, absently cupping her elbow or shoulder to get her attention.

'I can manage by myself you know,' she complained once, when he hefted her over a rocky outcrop with a hand splayed against her bottom.

'It's more fun this way,' he grinned, his hands falling away caressingly before he lifted Nic and climbed up himself.

Gina sniffed and he chuckled, putting his hand on her back to press her forward. 'I wouldn't have thought you were the type to go in for all this touching,' she said, moving her shoulders to shake him off, and then felt foolish at leaving herself open to another innuendo. But surprisingly he ignored the opening.

'Everyone needs physical affection,' he said softly, watching Nic negotiate the rock pools with alarming speed. 'But you're right, until now I haven't been much of a toucher. My own family were never ones to show their feelings, and Cyn hated having her hair ruffled or her clothes mussed by a hug.'

'So do I, sometimes,' said Gina, wondering why she was defending a woman that she didn't know, and wouldn't like if she did know.

'Very rarely, I should think. You're too aware of the preciousness of non-verbal communication to reject it out of hand. If you were like Cyn you wouldn't tumble around with Nic and put up with all the sand and grit in your clothes and half the island bush in your hair.' He plucked out a leaf and twirled it over her cheek, a familiar gleam entering his eyes as they came to a halt beside Nic, who was investigating a sea-urchin. 'You and my son both create a desire in me to touch just for the sake of touching another human being, of proving that I exist and that I'm not alone.'

He leaned forward and kissed her softly parted lips, gently and undemandingly. 'Loneliness is the worst punishment for our mistakes, and the most frequently self-inflicted.'

Gina put her hand to her lightly tingling mouth. 'What did you do that for?'

'For Nic.' The eyes were filled with sunlight and laughter. 'Isn't everything we do "for Nic"? To show him how harmless a kiss can be.'

'He's not even looking,' she managed to protest, moving away from the disturbingly hard body that had skimmed hers.

'I was just practising. In case I'd forgotten how,' he said outrageously.

He made sure he didn't forget. He kissed her quite often after that ... quick, stolen, unsatisfying kisses that lingered on her lips long after his warm, mobile mouth had left hers. She came to expect them, to aid and abet the thief, to close her eyes against where it was all leading.

She decided not to think ahead or let anything shadow the lazy pleasure of this holiday. She had sent a telegram to Daniel, not wanting to speak to him on the telephone or give him the opportunity of asking her any questions. Let him think she was still working on the book, she would cross the bridge of his angry disapproval later, when she had to.

One afternoon, as they set out to walk the entire three-mile length of the island, they passed the bungalow and Gina was surprised to see that although the place had been tidied up, no start had been made on repairs.

'I thought you'd got some building supplies in,' she said to Leo. 'Why haven't you started? Haven't you got the men?'

'Perhaps I don't want to risk having it finished,' he replied smoothly. 'In case you take it into your head to go back there.'

'It would hardly be worth it, I'm not going to be here much longer,' she said to punish him for the jolt of satisfaction that gave her.

'You keep saying that. But still you stay,' he taunted softly, restraining the urge to crush her pride by kissing her into senseless submission. His impatience was playing havoc with his self-control. If he hadn't possessed a sense of humour he would be out of his skull by now, trapped as he was in a permanent state of semi-arousal. Yet he knew the time wasn't ripe yet for him to make his move. She was still looking back over her shoulder, afraid of making another mistake. She would resent him taking her before she was ready, before she admitted the potent attraction that Leo was sure was obvious to everyone else at the villa except, possibly, Nic. She was a virgin, and Leo would be her first lover ... best lover, wiping out the fantasies of love with any other man. He would complete the awakening, set the seal of her desire with his body. There was more, but it could wait, and there were complications first to be resolved. The most important thing was to capture her imagination, her senses, to entice her softly into his arms, his bed, and let her discover there the explosive potential that she had so resolutely locked away. There would be freedom in his possession; he dared hope she might use it to claim a possession of her own. There could be a place in his life for this intriguing almost-woman if she chose to want it.

'Perhaps that's not so much because I want to stay,

but because I don't want to go home,' the perverse child was saying.

'Where is home? Do you still live with your mother, and *don't* stiffen up on me like that every time I mention your family.'

'I know what you think of them,' Gina said curtly as they forged through the bush, Nic singing an off-key advertising jingle ahead of them. He watched video-taped children's television programmes in the evenings, his hearing-aid looped into the VCR, but he seemed to prefer the short, snappy commercial breaks to the programmes themselves.

'Don't you think the same?' came the aggravatingly careful reply.

'They're still all the family I have.'

'Then why don't you want to go back to them?'

'I . . . I've lived at home too long. I suppose because it was safe, it was easy. Mother doesn't approve of what I do but she had a big studio converted there for me. I don't think I would have been able to cope out on my own.'

'Did *she* tell you that?' he asked perceptively. 'Why can you view her so clearly in some ways and so obscurely in others?'

'Because she's my mother, and I suppose I've never really outgrown the need for maternal approval,' she grimaced.

'I don't think it's something that anyone outgrows, unless they're completely callous. And, thank God, you're not that, Gina; but you *do* have a life of your own to live and you must see how impossible that will be to do in her shadow.'

'I won't ever become like them,' Gina said fiercely.

'No, I don't believe you will. But that won't stop your mother trying to draw you into her life. Why shouldn't she? For her it's a good life.'

It became imperative to explain, knowing that he was right. The way that Margaret had talked before Gina left for the island it sounded as if she had all sorts of plans for re-launching her youngest daughter into society.

'I planned on finding myself a flat somewhere when I went back,' she said haltingly. 'I . . . my father left me some money that I can use and my illustrating is just starting to pay really well so at least I don't have to beg her to bankroll me. With Margaret it's always better to act first and make excuses later, she doesn't believe in shedding tears over spilt milk. She'll probably enjoy telling everyone about her ungrateful daughter when she gets over the shock. In fact she'll probably secretly hope I run away with a penniless artist just to make an even more delicious scandal . . . a *proper* artist of course.'

He heard the wry bitterness. 'Don't you consider yourself an artist? Isn't what you do art?'

'Life is art,' Gina said flippantly, adding with a shrug, 'I haven't got the patience to work on a bigger scale.'

'I would have thought that what you do takes a great deal of patience. It's a virtue you must have had to cultivate very seriously over the last few years.'

The deep, slow, thoughtful tone refused to let her escape in light evasion. 'I . . . I took a few lessons with an art guild but I really just didn't seem to be able to take that step from drawing someone's words to creating——' she stopped as she saw his sceptical look. 'Oh, all right! I'm lazy. I like what I do and I don't crave to sign my name to a so-called piece of "great art", or struggle in obscurity because my work isn't "in". I have a very practical turn of mind, I like the appeal of a steady income—even if I don't need it—and I like the idea of my drawings being looked at and enjoyed simultaneously all over the world. Is that plebian enough for you? Have I shattered your illusion of me being a frustrated artist?'

His grin accepted her honesty and respected it before

he teased her out of her scowl. 'Not at all. I should hope that all your frustrations are centred in another sphere entirely.'

That was the last, uncomplicated afternoon they spent together before the blow fell, bringing Gina's lovely, unrealistic idyll to an abrupt end.

Returning from the swim with Nic the next morning, Leo having opted out to make a few business calls, Gina found herself wondering at his prolonged absence. He had said he was going to join them as soon as he had completed his calls but it was almost lunchtime. She sent Nic to change and slipped down to her room to pick through her own meagre wardrobe. She had written to her insurance company about the loss of her clothes and other possessions but in practical terms they had been unimportant. She wore a pareu or T-shirt and shorts or cotton jeans in the daytime and in the evening wore one of Liana's beautiful wrap-around dresses. It didn't seem to matter what she wore, Leo still looked at her with that same, penetrating intensity, as if he could see straight through her clothes anyway.

Gina stopped dead at the sight of the object of her thoughts stretched out on his back on her bed, his shoulders propped against the bamboo bedhead. Papers were scattered beside him. Familiar, typescript sheets of paper.

'What are you doing?' Gina croaked, her towel falling to the floor, her hair lying in damp snakes over the shoulders of a voluminous T-shirt that hid only a reasonably modest bikini bottom, she having rinsed off the top and a few ounces of sand under the cold shower outside the kitchen door.

'Doing what I do best, Ms Borelli. Assessing a manuscript.'

And not finding it very interesting, by the frigid tone of voice. Gina tried to recover her poise.

'How *dare* you go through my private things!'

'Private? How can something destined for publication be deemed "private"?'

'Is this the *business* you told us you had to do? Snooping in my room?' she demanded angrily, stepping closer, but not too close.

'Actually the room is mine, the villa is mine, the *island* is mine,' he pointed out, the coolness becoming ice-edged. 'And I'm reliably informed that this——' he lifted the sheets in his hand, '—is also mine.'

'Not until it's finished,' Gina snapped, backing into a corner.

'And when do you plan on finishing it, Ms Borelli?' he sneered. 'When do you plan to repay my company's hospitality with the fruits of your creative effort? From what I can see of these notes you haven't made a single one of the suggested revisions.'

'I . . . how did you find out?' she asked, subdued by the evident rage seething beneath the ice.

'My *business* included calling Kane to check that your illustrations had arrived. Imagine my surprise on being told that Sterne doesn't publish Gina Bennett books. Imagine my further surprise on being informed that the mysteriously non-existent G. Borelli is working on a novel—or *supposed* to be working on one.'

'I'm not writing to any deadline.'

'You mean you're not writing at all!'

'It's nothing to do with you.'

'Wrong! Everything to do with Sterne Publishing has to do with me.'

'I'm not under any contract!'

'No, but you did sign a document that gives Sterne the right to publish the completed manuscript.'

'It's not going to be completed!' she burst out, driven by this terse, cold-eyed stranger to blurt out the truth. He seemed to have a genius for making her reach down inside herself for what it was easier, less painful, to hide from general view.

'I see. Running away again, Gina? What an expert you're becoming at it. I thought you had more guts.'

She stiffened even further. 'What do you care about one book more or less? I don't owe you any explanations. Daniel is the only one I owe anything to.'

'Who's Daniel?' he demanded harshly, swinging his legs off the bed, still holding part of her manuscript in one hand while his body blocked her off from the rest of it.

'My . . . my editor, my agent, my *friend*. He's the one who wants this published, not me!'

'Why?'

'Why? Why do you think! Because he thought it was good.'

'This?' Instead of getting up and towering angrily over her he was suddenly lounging back on one hand, the other holding the manuscript away from his body as if it was a primed grenade. 'This self-indulgent posturing?'

Gina felt as if he'd thrown a bucket of water over her. He hated it, just as she thought he would. Instead of feeling pleased at his giving her a cast iron excuse to give up the painful project she had thoughtlessly thrown herself into, she felt her temper rise several notches.

'Daniel thinks it's good . . . so does your Kane.'

'Good? Oh, yes, it'll sell all right. The over-emotional, under-developed teenage market always loves a good tear-jerker.'

'That's just a first draft.'

'But you said you weren't going to finish it. So it stands or falls on what it is now . . . a piece of over-written, flatulent, poorly constructed melodrama.'

She snatched the manuscript from his hand and held it defensively to her chest, furious with him for dismissing the torments of her soul with such scathing cruelty. Only moments ago he had been angry and she had expected him to try and force her to continue the book.

'I didn't ask for your opinion! Have you ever written a book? No! All you do is criticise the work of other people. That's easy . . . even *I* can do that. This may not be great writing but it's only a first attempt and I did it on my own with no help from anyone. I don't care what *you* think.'

'Then why is your voice cracking up?'

'Because you make me so mad, that's why!' she hissed at him. 'How dare you come in here and——'

'Tell the truth? Are you furious with me for being honest, or for being right? Do you want me to praise you, to tell you that you've written the definitive New Zealand novel . . .?'

'No!'

'Then what do you want, Gina? To throw it away?'

'No!' She hugged it more tightly against her as he got up, his face no longer taunting but intent, reserved.

'Why not?' he asked quietly. 'It's certainly never going to go anywhere in its present form. You can go back to your illustrating, that nice, proven money-spinner and forget you ever came close to creating something beautiful and enduring out of an emotional disaster.' He bent, not taking his eyes off her pale face, and picked up a single sheet from the bed and tore it across.

'No!' Gina stared at the torn pieces, amazed at the shock it gave her.

'No. You can't let me destroy it, Gina . . . you can't destroy it yourself. You've created something. It exists. It has a hold on you that you'll never shake, not until you finish it. The creative urge is like that . . . persistent, tenacious, possessive. Your drawings are your children, Gina, and this is your child too, even if you consider it a bastard.' His mouth quirked. 'In more ways than one.'

'Are you telling me to . . . to keep going?' Gina asked, dazed by this sudden change from insult to insidious gentleness. 'According to you it's not worth working on.'

'Did I say that?'

'I ...' She frowned. She couldn't remember exactly what he had said, only that fierce urge to protect what was hers. Confusedly she felt him ease the manuscript out of her clenched fingers and put it behind him, but when he took her shoulders in a firm grip she struggled. 'Let me go.'

'No.' He calmed her resistance. 'Not you and not that book. You're going to write it for me, Gina.' He tilted her chin up and looked at her with a tender implacability. 'And for you ... and for Nic ... and all those people who think that they are less than whole and therefore think that they deserve less than love.'

'I don't think I can,' she whispered, dark eyes pleading, but his determination fed on her uncertainty.

'I do. I was an editor before I became the owner of a publishing business. I know exactly what Kane was trying to get you to do through those notes of his. I see the basis of a strong plot overwhelmed by the emotions of the writer, I see fine writing floundering for lack of direction, I see inconsistencies and distortions in your characters that don't work within the context of your story. How long did it take you to write?'

'A few months,' Gina said huskily, overwhelmed herself at the extent of his criticism, and even more dubious about the task he wanted to set her. 'I didn't have any work lined up for after the operation and I couldn't bear just sitting around brooding so ...' She shrugged and moved out of his hands to slowly gather up some of the scattered paper from the bed, thereby avoiding his direct gaze.

'You just sat down and wrote?'

'Sort of. I used to keep a diary, a kind of outlet I suppose, for all the things I couldn't say out loud. I drew from that for my central character, for Marina's stream-of-consciousness bits. The rest grew up around it.'

'So the first half of the book—Marina's experiences

growing up after the accident in which she lost her voice, they're very much factual?' Gina nodded, putting the stack of papers on the bedside table. 'And the second half, where she meets Malcolm, is also based in fact . . . but far more loosely?'

'Yes.' He must know it was true, so why was he forcing her to admit it?

'That's the part that needs the most work. It needs to be pared down so that the characters are allowed to reveal their motivations through their words and actions rather than thrusting them down the readers' throats.'

'I . . . I wouldn't know how——' Gina began feebly.

'Then let me show you. Work with me. All those things I said about the book were true, but it's also true that I agree with Kane's assessment of your potential. It would be a shame to waste it.'

'But when . . .?'

'It's about time Nic began to face more of *his* responsibilities. Miss Hamilton seems to think he's ready to cope with a full afternoon of lessons each day. You can write in the evenings and we can use those few hours in the day to examine and discuss what you're doing.'

'I might disappoint you,' Gina murmured, frightened and at the same time oddly elated by his confidence.

'That's a risk publishers take every time they sign a new writer.'

'You're very clever,' she said, suddenly seeing things clearly for the first time since she had entered the room. She tossed back her rapidly-drying hair and gave him a glare of grudging admiration. 'You meant me to get angry, didn't you?'

'In spite of your insecurities you rise very passionately to your own defence,' he agreed with a golden smile, once more the pleasant companion of the last few days. 'I can't fight you when you're all sad, dark-eyed vulnerability, but when you're spitting mad I don't feel the need to pull my punches, or protect you from yourself. You're stronger than you realise, Gina, and I intend to prove it.'

Prove it he did, with a stubborn relentlessness that thwarted every attempt at slackness. Nic provided no excuses for Gina to cry off the traumatic daily sessions in Leo's room. After a mild fit of the sulks he had adjusted to the new routine far better than Gina. Once his father explained that Gina was working on a book, he too decided that he was going to write a book— about being deaf—and was cunningly persuaded that Miss Hamilton would make the best possible editor. *My* editor and *your* editor, he gigglingly referred to his teacher and his father and surprisingly his enthusiasm didn't flag even as he struggled with the alien concepts of grammar and spelling.

During her first afternoon with Leo in his role as editor Gina sat appalled as he stripped her manuscript down to the bone, running a lightning pencil through whole pages of sweated labour.

'It's too long,' was all he said when she protested.

By the second day Gina had decided that if she didn't stand up for herself he was going to totally change the character of the book. At his criticism of the way the book ended she flared defiantly.

'It's *supposed* to be a tragedy,' she snapped across the desk at him. 'I refuse to let them all live happily ever after just to satisfy your obsession with loose ends.'

'The tragedy is inherent in the situation,' he replied with the calmness that characterised all his dealings with her book. There was something paternal about his attitude that was almost as annoying as his constant criticism. 'It's this insistence of yours on hammering the point constantly home that turns tragedy into melo-drama. You spend the first half of the book showing us the slow and difficult emergence of a strong individual who is forced to reassess everything she has been taught about life and who learns, through her suffering, to

cope with pressures that would have previously crushed
her. Yet you also ask us to believe that this is the kind
of woman who would commit suicide. I don't believe it.
She might consider it, yes—there's a point of despair
when all of us would—but never choose it over life. Not
after what she had already endured to preserve and
enhance the life she has. She would go on, disillusioned,
bitter perhaps, but she would go on.'

'But she loved Malcolm, what he did shattered her
strength. It was the last straw——'

'As Niven was the last straw for you? You didn't
commit suicide. Did *you* think about it?'

Not for an instant. She had been too angry. 'I'm not
Marina. I got my voice back ... she never would
have——'

'You didn't know at that stage that you *were* getting
yours back.' His golden gaze was probing, intent. 'Even
at the moment that she realises how she has been used,
Marina also faces the truth of Malcolm's worthlessness.
Is she going to also give him the final victory? Is she
going to give him her life as well as her love? You
didn't, neither would she.'

'It's the whole point of the book.'

'Only because you make it so, and force everything
else to fit into the straitjacket. Why? Not because the
book demands it. Are you trying perhaps to punish
Niven in some obscure way? A kind of "if I died he'd be
sorry"?'

A mist rose in front of Gina's eyes, hazing her
vision along with her thoughts as she listened
helplessly to the searingly accurate exposure of her
most secret feelings.

'In the same way you've made Malcolm an unrelieved
villain, whereas you must know that such people are
extremly rare, and quite unbelievable in fiction. His
own actions condemn him, you don't have to stress
them, and he too should possess conflicts in his
character. He's in love with this other woman as far as

it is possible for him to love anyone. That doesn't excuse the way he used Marina, but it does explain it. The real tragedy is the realisation of how completely random our chances for happiness . . . or for bitter grief . . . are. But it's how we accept the fall of the cards that really shapes our future.'

'You think I should forgive him, don't you?' whispered Gina, sifting through the layers of meaning in that soft velvet voice.

'You? I thought we were talking about Marina.'

There was a stricken silence. 'You do this to me deliberately,' she accused wearily, at last.

'Only to make you think about what you're writing and why. And maybe you do have to forgive him, Gina, or you'll never be able to forgive yourself for not seeing him for what he was until too late.'

She would never be able to forgive him. Never! Grimly Gina drove herself to re-work some of the more difficult passages in the book, finding her perceptions sharpened by the chill wind of Leo's trenchant opinions. Yet even as she fought his interpretation she found herself being influenced by it. What was emerging from the borrowed electronic typewriter was a shorter, yet more complex, version of the original. And better, much better.

Needing, but also resenting this invasion into her private world made Gina defensively peevish. She didn't want Leo to guess that part of her resentment stemmed from his apparent ability to switch off his personal awareness of her each time they sat down at his desk. She couldn't do that, couldn't stop the restless need to provoke and annoy him that invaded her at every turn. All she got in return were metaphorical pats on the head and when her peevishness invaded their hours with Nic the two males were disgustingly tolerant. Everything seemed to be going swimmingly for Leo. Now it was Gina's turn to feel at odds with the world.

One evening, fed up with being ignored in favour of

the monster she had created, Gina slammed down her hands on the typewriter keys and stood up.

'I'm not doing any more tonight. And furthermore I am not going to change a word of what I wrote yesterday!'

Leo looked up from the page he was reading, lounging back in the chair, his feet propped up on the other side of the desk. 'Fine.'

'Fine? Fine!' Gina was enraged. 'Is that all you can say ... after all those pin-pricking points you raised this afternoon!'

'You need the services of a devil's advocate to shift that lazy backside of yours into gear,' he grinned. 'Besides, I like to watch you work yourself into a rage.'

'You——' Gina misplaced her voice at the critical moment and compensated by picking up the empty coffee cup from the desk and throwing it at him. He ducked and the cup shattered against the wall behind him.

He laughed, and nearly tipped off the chair as he tried to avoid another missile. 'Now, Gina——'

'You like to watch me in a rage,' she whispered raggedly, 'well watch this!' He stopped laughing as she picked up a heavy paperweight and stood up warily.

'You don't really want to hurt me do you, gypsy, you just want my attention,' he said softly, with aggravating perception.

The paperweight flew and Gina's hands flew to her mouth in horror at what she'd done. He avoided it, just, and advanced towards her threateningly. 'Well, now you have it, all of it. What are you going to do with it?' Gina looked wildly around her and his eyes glimmered narrowly. 'If you're looking for something else to throw at me, darling, how about yourself?'

Leo, she mouthed pleadingly at him, her hands spread in a gesture of submission, dismayed at the result of her swift burst of temper, at the speed of his reaction.

'Lost your voice again? How timely.' He snatched her

against him and held her tightly against the lean, hard body. 'You don't want to fight, you want to make love, that's what's making you so scratchy. Are you ready for me now, Gina? Ready for a lover?'

She shook her head mutely, trying to deny the tingling that presaged an explosion deep inside her and he chuckled in a voice as husky as the one that lurked in her throat. 'I said all you ever had to say was no, but you can't say it, can you? No words, Gina, so I'll have to read what your body tells me.' He moved his pelvis against her and she felt the force and heat of his desire and almost melted at the knees as he backed her over to the large, inviting bed. 'Let me teach you the exquisite language of love, let me be your interpreter. Let me show you how fluent you can be with the right man.'

He kissed her and she trembled, excited, impatient, as he pressed her into the cool softness of the bed, all her anger revealing itself as a different kind of passion. She clung and moved with him and he kissed her more deeply, his hands moving over her, pulling off her clothes to bare the silk and satin of her body, stripping off his own. He knelt beside her and stroked her calves, her thighs, buried his face between her breasts as he touched her with an intimacy that stunned her. She seemed to have no will but to please him, no modesty, no shame. She let him praise her body with his mouth and the disturbing skill of his fingers, she let him look his fill at her shuddering desire and gloried in the sight of the honey-soft hair brushing her skin, the tanned flesh against her where she was creamy pale.

He lay beside her and the slow, languorous exploration became fused with a taut expectation that filled Gina with a sensual apprehension. Not content with arousing her to blind delight, Leo urged her to arouse him, stroked himself with her hands, told her where to press her kisses, how to move her hips and long golden legs to give them both pleasure. Gina became possessed of a hunger for completion that banished whatever fear or shyness had remained.

'Leo, please ...' she captured her elusive voice to whisper against his hard shoulder and he gave a husky groan against her mouth, his hands tightening on her breasts in a gentle milking motion that made her gasp.

'Don't use words, darling, show me ... show me what you want ... open yourself to me, Gina, don't hold back.'

Her hands dug into his back as she arched her buttocks off the bed to push against his maleness, feeling the hot thrust of him between her thighs and obeying the instinct to draw him down to her.

He was groaning now as he balanced on the two-edged sword, trying to rein himself back to draw out her pleasure but finding that in doing so he was increasing his own to uncontrollable proportions. In the end his own skill defeated him.

Driven wild by violent sensation Gina engulfed him with greedy compliance, oblivious to any discomfort, only marvelling at the strange new sensation of being filled to bursting point, of being anchored to that thrusting, heaving male body, of being held tight and hard in the grip of a dance of the flesh that spun her higher and faster to a music she had never heard before. As her eyes widened with the wondrous knowledge of delight she saw the masculine face poised above her, its passionate, pagan beauty surpassing the physical. She saw the golden head go back, the lashes flicker against drawn cheeks, his teeth clench against an anguished sound and then he ignited her with a flame that consumed them both and fused the moment into fiery victory.

CHAPTER NINE

'Good morning.'

Disturbed from a deliciously dreamless sleep Gina frowned, her eyelids fluttering as she burrowed her face deeper into her pillow. Then she became aware that the pillow was hard, rather than soft, and warm and alive under her cheek. Her eyes flew open, her head lifting.

'Good morning.'

She stared at the lazy lion in bed beside her, his golden strength relaxed as he smiled warmly into her astonished face. It took only a moment for astonishment to turn into remembrance.

'G ... good morning,' she whispered uncertainly.

'I kept my promise, you see,' he murmured, the muscles shifting across his shoulders as he propped himself up on an elbow, his other hand on her waist when she would have edged away. 'I brought you back to your own room.'

Gina realised belatedly that they were in her bed, not his, and she threw a nervous look at the door. 'I didn't mean you to come too,' she rasped, frustrated by her early morning inability to get the words out easily. 'Nic usually comes in when he wakes up.'

'That's why I woke you,' he said, dipping his head to place a light kiss against her furrowed brow. 'It's barely dawn. Nic won't wake up for a while yet.'

'Oh.' Gina swallowed, not knowing what to make of his tenderness. Had he woken her so that they could make love again? In the warm nest of the bed she shivered with anticipation. After that first explosive coming together he had taken her again, this time in a different way ... very slowly, almost lazily, a long, leisurely journey which had terminated in a way even more glorious than the first. She had fallen asleep in his arms and he must have carried her in here. Would the third time be even better still? Would it always get better and better? Had he felt any of the shattering joy that she had? Or was he too blasé about sex to share the kind of incredulous delight that she had felt?

'Having regrets?' he asked softly, disconcerting her further.

'Regrets?'

'That the loss of your virginity wasn't accompanied by more ceremony?'

She blushed faintly while her eyes widened at his quizzical expression. Was that diffidence she heard in his voice? Was Leo actually asking *her* ...? 'I think I had all the ceremony that I could handle,' she said with shy frankness. 'I ... is it always so ...?'

'So what?' His mouth curved sensuously, satisfaction gleaming in the golden eyes, his unspoken question answered by the curiosity that conquered her uncertainty. His hand tightened on her waist as he drew their bodies together, enjoying the way her colour fluctuated and her eyes avoided his while her silky-warm body curved instinctively into his.

'So ...' Her mouth went dry as she felt the roughness of his thighs nudge hers, the intimate way their hips moulded together, the way her breasts tightened against his chest.

'So what?' he urged softly, stroking at her parted lips with his tongue, inserting it to slowly taste her morning sweetness. He pushed her on to her back and bent over her to deepen the kiss, pushing the sheet down to her waist and then lifting his head to enjoy the sight of her roused breasts, her slightly swollen reddened mouth and the laquered black glaze of her eyes. 'So ... what?' he asked hungrily.

'So... beautiful, so fierce.' Her voice was thick with dreams. 'So like, like ...'

'Like nothing else on earth; yes, with the right

partner it can always be like that,' he said, unable to prevent his hand going out to take firm possession of her breast. Gina felt its weight as she felt the weight of his words on her ears, as a statement of intent. Only, intention for what? She trembled under his touch and saw that he was pleased by it.

'Perhaps, after a while, the sense of urgency may not be the same, but when mind and sense are engaged repetition can only enhance lovemaking. It's self-renewing and self-fulfilling. Each time I kiss you I want to touch you, each time I touch you I want to make love to you, each time I make love to you I want to do it again.' His hands moved on her, drawing her back down into that sensual world that he had discovered for her and Gina went willingly, without regret, discovering it all over again and revelling in the bright newness of it.

She winced as his hand found her and he paused. 'Tender? I'll be very, very gentle, darling. Trust me ... that's right ... come where I lead ...' He wound a spell around her with his coaxing words, and wove an even more blindingly beautiful one with the feathery curiosity of his fingers. He was so gentle it was like being possessed by the breeze, but a hot, silky, stroking breeze that excited rather than soothed which found its way into every crevasse, which fanned a steady smoulder into a brief and incandescent flare.

'Don't you prefer me to Nic as a morning alarm?' he murmured afterwards into her flushed and dewy face.

'I don't know,' she found the breath to tease him in return. 'Nic makes me feel like getting up, you make me ...'

He stroked a finger across her damp brow, his face almost boyishly smooth in its contentment. 'Want to stay in bed all day? The feeling is entirely mutual, my little no-so-innocent.'

'But it's different for you,' she said, fingering the sheet he had tucked up around them again.

'You mean because I've done it all before?' he asked in a voice filled with amusement. 'But I haven't—not with you. In fact you seem to have a rather inflated opinion of my expertise.' His amusement slid into ruefulness. 'It does my ego no end of good, but I'm bound by my sense of fair play to disillusion you. I'm no stud.'

'Oh, really?' Gina allowed herself a moment of revenge, her lashes hiding her mischief. 'You mean if I found a stud he'd make me feel even better than you did.'

'No, that's not what I——' he began roughly, eyes narrowing as he noticed the tilt of her mouth. 'Damn you, gypsy girl, don't tease me.'

'You tease me,' she pointed out.

'Only because I'm afraid to come on too strong for you. You're wary of men, quite rightly. Stay that way, except with me.'

'Why should you be the exception?' she demanded, stiffening against him. Did he think that, given half the chance, she'd be as promiscuous as her sisters?

'Because I care what happens to you,' he said, pinning her to the bed with his look. 'Because you're rare, and precious, a dark jewel among a tawdry glitter that surrounds you.' His hand stroked her hair as she lay, stunned by the thick intensity of his words and then it moved to her throat and his voice hardened. 'And perhaps you'll hate me for saying this but what's purest male in me is glad that you let these stand guard over your innocence, that you never had the voice to say to any man what you say to me. Is that cruel? I can be crueller still: I'm even glad that Niven hurt you, because I reaped what he sowed. The first, best harvest. No other man shall ever have that privilege. You gave it to me.'

Gina was fighting for breath, feeling strangely frightened by the way he spoke. She should hate him for what he said, not feel this wrenching sweetness. She laid a hand against his, pressing it into her throat, meeting the angry challenge in his eyes with one of her own.

'And what do you offer me, in exchange?'

His eyes blazed briefly. 'Whatever you ask for, Gina. Whatever you *dare* to ask for.'

She was about to ask him, puzzled, what he meant when there was a slight sound from the next room.

'It's Nic!'

They looked at each other for a frozen moment, like a pair of guilty children.

'You have to go,' Gina said, although all she wanted was to stay here, bound to his strength, exploring the deeper implications of what they had done together.

'I agree . . . this time,' he warned her, low-voiced, as he got out of bed and stretched, unashamed of his nakedness. He picked up a dark blue robe that was tossed across the end of the bed and slid his arms into the loose sleeves. 'But sooner or later he's going to have to know.'

'Why?' Gina asked, distracted by the heat in her belly at the sight of the masculinity he was shrouding in blue silk.

'Why!' He looked annoyed at her question. 'Did you think we were going to pretend that nothing has happened between us? That we're going to confine our relationship as lovers to sneaking around under cover of darkness?'

'I . . . I don't know.' Gina hitched the sheet up awkwardly. 'I never thought about it.'

'Well, I did.' Hands on hips he towered at the end of the bed with the confidence of someone who is not going to be denied. 'We're both adults, we don't have to hide our feelings, or make excuses for them. Believe me, Gina, you'd find it very difficult to dissemble. Making love irrevocably alters any relationship and Nic has learned to be very observant, he'll notice any attempt at constraint on your part. If you're less spontaneous in expressing yourself he'll be suspicious ... and he'll inevitably connect it with me.'

'He seems much more ready to accept you.'

'Not quite yet, it's still in the balance ... it could tip either way. But this has more to do with you than with Nic. I won't have you feeling that I regret in any way making love to you, or think any less of you for sharing my desire. If you're going to argue about this, Gina, I'll get right back into bed with you and we'll tell Nic *now* that you and I are cementing our bond of friendship as adult men and women do, through loving, and that he is part of that loving.'

'That's a beautiful way of putting it,' said Gina throatily. It struck her that in spite of his failure in the past, an inexperience at being a father, he had the instinct deep within him that would make him a good one.

'The truth often is beautiful.'

'Leo ...' her whisper stopped him as he turned away. 'I ... thank you ... you made it very ... special.'

'It will always be special between us, Gina. You're very passionate and you have a lovely body.'

Her blushing reply came as he opened the door. 'I ... I love your body, too.'

He gave her one, last, lazy look that she was unable to interpret. 'Well, that's a start, anyway.'

Gina didn't have long to ponder the cryptic murmur. Nic joined her shortly afterwards and she found herself seeing him with new eyes. Her lover's child. His mother must be dark, for he hadn't inherited that colouring from his father. She wondered fleetingly whether her child by Leo would be dark and then pushed the thought aside. There would be no child, dark or otherwise. Last night, somewhere in the midst of that heated seduction, Leo had asked her if she was protected and she had told him that she was on the pill, prescribed to control her irregular periods. Leo obviously didn't want any unnecessary complications, and neither did Gina. She just wanted to enjoy the moment and not think of the future.

If she had thought to dissemble, the next few days showed her how impossible that would have been. Her sense of physical well-being permeated her entire personality, giving her a poise and self-confidence that she had previously only possessed in regard to her work. And all this because of a *man*. Niven had never given her this feeling. Their romantic little subterfuges had made her feel illicit excitement but she had never felt this freedom to express herself, this delightful combination of lassitude and energy. Instead of embarrassing her, Liana's warm, knowing smiles only made her want to laugh, and Aileen Hamilton's placid acceptance of her employer's attitude of relaxed intimacy with the latest member of the household succeeded in making Gina feel even more at home in her unfamiliar role as mistress. She refused to entertain the thought that Aileen's acceptance might be due more to the fact that she was used to women coming and going than to the fact that it was Gina.

Although Leo was tender, passionate, teasing and demanding by turns during their free time together, he was still a slave-driver when it came to her book. In fact he seemed more determined than ever to squeeze the best out of her, and didn't allow her to get away with trying to distract him.

'Stop it, Gina, and get your mind on what you're supposed to be doing,' he growled at her one afternoon as she stared at him dreamily over the top of her typewriter, trying to see if she could disturb him as he did her . . . with a mere look.

'Stop what?' she asked innocently blinking at him.

'Stop looking at me like that.'

'I was thinking,' she protested, a tiny curve of her mouth tempting him to respond.

'Yes, and I know what you were thinking about,' he said coolly, refusing to play.

'Can you read my mind?' Gina leant back in her chair, flexing her shoulders so that her breasts jutted out against the cotton T-shirt, round and firm and wanting his touch.

'I read your eyes, your mouth,' the golden gaze flickered briefly down, 'your body ... our non-verbal communication is very good. But no sex, Gina, until you've finished this chapter.'

'That's blackmail,' said Gina, trying to control a vivid blush and not quite succeeding. She couldn't quite get used to Leo's boldness, his honest approach to sex. In her sisters' circles it was all wrapped up in tinsel paper, outwardly blatant but so crammed with game-and role-playing that the contents were incomprehensible.

'It's common sense,' came the velvet reply. 'If I started to make love to you now I wouldn't be able to stop. And once wouldn't be enough. With you and me it never is. We'd spend all afternoon in bed. Pleasurable, but hardly profitable.'

'And you expect me to work *now*?' said Gina faintly, her hands trembling so much she doubted they would find the typewriter keys. How could he say things like that and look so unmoved by the images he created between them?

He watched her for a moment, as she sought for control and when she had almost achieved it he smiled a wicked smile. 'If you do well this afternoon, Gina, tonight I'll try something a little more inventive. I think you'll like it.'

'You devil!' she told him shakily, swallowing, and summoning back the reluctant desire to work with an effort of will. *More* inventive? What he had shown her already had been mind-bending enough. How much more pleasure could her body stand! 'If you're trying to get my mind back on this manuscript you're going the wrong way about it.'

'Try putting some of that passion down on paper,' he

told her, returning to his editing of her previous day's writing, obviously regretting his momentary lapse. He had told Gina that he intended, in the future, to concentrate on running his publishing business ... was he using her as a means of getting back into shape? Sharpening his critical faculties on the whetstone of her book? He certainly seemed to enjoy what he was doing and he had made Gina enjoy it too, in a punishing sort of way.

Unfortunately Nic seemed extremely suspicious of the disturbing new aspects of their relationship and seemed to have returned, rather half-heartedly, to a few of his old tricks, but when Gina expressed her worry to Leo he said calmly,

'He'll work it through. It's natural for him to feel a bit threatened, but he'll settle down when he sees that it doesn't change things for *him*.'

'Perhaps we should stop——'

'No way, Gina,' came the forceful answer. 'We've created something between us with this affair that, like that book of yours, can't be sent back into limbo. Nic's intelligence will soon reason out that whatever it is that binds you to me must also therefore bind you to him, and he'll be glad of it.'

As their physical intimacy deepened, so Leo encouraged an intimacy of the mind that Gina found both stimulating and comforting. He listened to her talk about her long unexpressed feelings and helped her to a deeper understanding of herself.

'You feel you let your mother down by being injured?' he asked when she told him about her reasonless guilt over the accident.

'In a way. She doesn't like illness of any kind—I made her feel uncomfortable, which made me feel as if I was failing. Then again, I *was* a spoilt bitch in those days, self-pity made me feel important.' She told him about the social worker who had rescued her. 'He was terribly thick-skinned and a bully, but it worked.'

'Up to a point.' Leo grazed his mouth across her smooth forehead, inhaling the flowery fragrance of her hair. 'But a part of you still suffers from feeling unworthy, that's why you were such easy prey for Niven. Maybe you *did* see him for what he was but thought that was all you deserved.'

He was uncomfortably close to the truth that Gina had come to face about herself and still wasn't ready to express.

'It's not such a bad thing, you know, to disappoint people with unreasonable expectations of what you should be,' he continued, his arms tightening around her, drawing her protectively against him and using her warmth as a buffer against his own unpleasant memories. 'Living up to them can be even more bitter. My mother worked herself into exhaustion after my father died, to scrape up the money to give me an education. No son of hers was going to spend all his life in the freezing works, hauling meat carcasses. She never had much of a life with Dad and I think she channelled all her thwarted ambitions through me. She *made* me want to be somebody for her sake, to give her everything she denied herself for years for her only son. Only she died before I clawed my way up. All she saw were the struggles and the setbacks, and she hated the way I pursued Cynthia ... said it would only bring me grief. She died not knowing whether all her sacrifices had been worth while. And she *needn't* have died, if some of the money she had earned working double-shifts in a factory had been spent on herself instead of me. Hackneyed as it may sound she literally worked herself into the grave. And I let her.'

'I'm sure it was worth it, to her.' Gina laid her head against the ruffled fur on his chest, wishing she could erase that bitterness from his voice, understanding it completely. 'She had her belief in you and it gave her something to live for, to strive for.'

'To die for?'

'Do you blame yourself for that?'

'In my lucid moments, no, it was her choice to bring me up in the way that she did. But, like you, I have those other moments, when I look at Nic and wonder what it's all for. Would she have been proud of her oh-so-successful and ambitious son if she had seen the way he treated his *own* son? And I swore, when I was still a teenager, that I would never make the mistake of trying to live through my children. Instead I went to the other extreme, and rejected parenthood altogether. Think of all the years that I have missed, the growing years, the learning years, Nic's *hearing* years.'

'And think of all the years to come.' Gina twisted her body so that she could look up at him, her eyes black with compassion. 'At least you're willing to learn from your mistakes.'

Then, to banish the bleakness from his eyes she began to make love to him, using all her untutored skill, and he let her torment them both with her hands and body before he exploded into action and revealed a new part of himself. Always before there had been an edge of tenderness in their lovemaking, a deference to her innocence. This time there was none. It was rough, almost hurting, and quickly over and yet afterwards Gina felt more loved than ever before. This time he had lost control completely and somehow that made Gina feel a kind of pride. He trusted her enough to cast the golden mask aside and let her see the naked passion beneath.

The next day came the confrontation that Gina had waited for, and feared. After a morning of energetic activity on the beach Nic baulked at being taken back to the villa to clean up for lunch and lessons.

I don't have to do what you say, you're not my mother, Nic signed jerkily at Gina, who paled at the wounding truth. At times she *felt* like his mother.

'Apologise to Gina, Nic,' his father said, a tightness in his voice that signalled to Gina that he was not going to let this pass, as he had other minor discourtesies and disobedience during the morning. She moved restlessly, not wanting to be the reason for their conflict. 'Stay where you are, Gina. I need you.'

She subsided instantly, aligned by his side, facing Nic, seeing the unhappiness in the dark young eyes, and the tension in the tiny clenched fists at his side. Nic, too, was spoiling for this.

She's not my mother, Nic signed again, his fingers as stiff as his face, obviously too wrought up for speech.

'No. But your mother isn't here, Nic, and Gina is,' Leo signed as he spoke, carefully and clearly. This was too important to let Nic miss a word. 'I thought you liked her, and wanted me to like her too. If I was wrong, I'm sorry.'

Nic frowned blackly, disconcerted by this turn of events. Did this mean that his father would go back to being horrid to Gina if Nic wanted him to? But he didn't. He wanted . . . he wanted . . .

'I love you, Nic. I want you to be happy here with me. I thought Gina was part of that happiness.' Not taking his eyes off his son he reached out and took Gina's hand, linking them together. 'Gina loves you too. She would be sad if you didn't want her here with us. I would be sad too, because she is special to me, as special as you are in a different way. You're my son, and nothing can ever change that. I want you to live where I live, go where I go, join in doing the things that I do.'

Gina held her breath as Nic looked stonily at their clasped hands and then intently into his father's face, searching for a flicker of insincerity. He found none. The golden eyes were steady, clear, holding a promise that Nic hardly dared let himself believe.

Mummy said you wouldn't want me. Mummy said you were too busy to want a boy who wasn't clever. He broke into speech, barely understandable, thick as it was with stubbornly unshed tears. 'She said you'd send me away

if I wasn't good, but you didn't ... why did she say
that? She said you never wanted to be anyone's Daddy
... you never wanted *me* at all, only your friends.'

Leo wrenched his hand out of Gina's and dropped on
his knees beside his son, taking him into his arms,
hugging him fiercely. There was exultation of his face,
but a haunting sadness too, at so much pain stored in
so small a body. Gina left them there, comforting each
other, longing to have the right to add her comfort too,
but knowing that they needed to be alone.

It was at dinner that they reappeared, wearing
identical expressions of self-conscious smugness.
Although both were quiet and undemonstrative, Gina
sensed an ease between them that had not existed
before. It looked as if all Leo's manoeuvring and hard
work had finally paid off.

Later, when he told Gina some of what Nic had
revealed—filling in the gaps from his knowledge of
Cynthia—she realised what a heavy load the boy had
carried, and why life must have seemed so utterly
bewildering to him.

Apparently, and understandably, all through his
babyhood Nic had heard over and over from his
mother that his father was working, and couldn't spend
time with them. When the split came, Cynthia had been
unable to hide her resentment and told him baldly that
his father didn't want him. Yet, as a behaviour control,
she also told him that if he was good Daddy would be
proud of him. After he became deaf, and his emotional
problems increased, there was still another variation:
she would send him to live with Daddy if he was bad,
and Daddy would be ashamed.

'No wonder the poor kid went crazy around me,' Leo
said as they lay together in his bed. 'Daddy was both
bribe and threat. Cynthia changed her mind so often he
never knew whether I was a monster or someone to try
to emulate. She would run me down to him and then
feel guilty and try and tell him how wealthy and

important I was. After the trauma of his illness he thought his deafness was something *he* had done, you know, shut out the world because it was too confusing. When it sank in that it wasn't, and he began to realise how his not being able to hear had made Cynthia react he thought I would never want him. I guess he got angry at the whole world and then, when he was sent to me, he thought it was yet another punishment. His resentment conflicted with his desperate desire to be wanted, to have a parent who was proud of him.' He cursed. 'Cynthia and her damned perfect world. If she had been less afraid of admitting failures I might have known sooner. I could have done something.'

'You couldn't have prevented his deafness,' said Gina quietly.

'No, but I could have prevented a lot of his unhappiness.'

'And now?'

'And now,' Leo smiled wryly. 'We start from the beginning again. For all the problems Cynthia created she's still his mother and up until now the only tiny piece of security he's known. Given the choice, he might prefer to return to her.'

'But I thought you had custody now? Would you let him go back?'

'No, but I don't want him to know that just yet, not until he comes to trust me more. And there are still . . . some things to be settled with regard to Cynthia and me.'

His tone didn't invite questions so Gina asked none. 'But from the way you talked . . . would she *want* him back?'

'I don't know. I don't know her any more, if I ever did. If she starts to feel guilty she might convince herself she ought to try again. If I can hold her off long enough, though, I think she'll accept she's not cut out to be a mother. She doesn't have patience. It's no slur on her as a woman, if she would only realise it. Some people just aren't cut out to be parents.'

'You are,' Gina told him confidently. 'You might have taken a while to accept it yourself, but I think you'll be a great father for Nic.'

'As great a father as I am a lover?' His eyes slitted at her.

'Nothing could be that great,' Gina responded instantly to his teasing, her husky laugh delighting him with its frank seduction, drawing him down again to her, enticing him to provide the proof of her words.

Now, even when they were with Nic, he felt no need to deny himself the pleasure of acknowledging her charms. In fact, he drew his son into the act, commenting to him how pretty Gina looked, or that she was putting on weight, or losing it. Gina laughed and played them at their own game, treating them both like cute little boys and trying not to blush as she detected the heated sincerity underlining Leo's teasing.

'I think you only insist we spend the morning on the beach so that you can watch me strip off,' she said to him one day, as he lay back on his towel and smiled at the provocative way she slid out of her pareu to reveal a tiny bikini underneath, her swimwear having become progressively more daring as her confidence rose in her own attractiveness.

'How did you guess?' he grinned wolfishly, and threw a glance to one side to make sure that Nic was out of lip-reading range. The boy had begun to reveal an embarrassing adeptness, giving further weight to Aileen Hamilton's opinion that he had been hiding his shining light under a bushel. 'Damn Nic. I want you here, now, on the sand. The way I wanted you that first night.'

'Getting bored with the bedroom?' she twinkled at him, bending over to arrange her towel so that he got an eyeful of her generous cleavage, then stretched out beside him.

'Not when you're in it,' he said so silkily that her

body tightened and he gave a stifled chuckle of sensual satisfaction. 'Your nipples are hard.'

Gina jammed on her hat, flushing, and the chuckle turned into a laugh.

'You can blush? After the way you carry on between the sheets! I never know who I'm going to find in my bed at night—a sultry, sexy gypsy who drives me wild with her lust, or a wide-eyed child-woman who giggles when I try to teach her something new.'

'I never know myself,' admitted Gina, feeling the familiar, silvery liquid of delight tracing through her veins. 'I never imagined it could be like this.'

'What could be like what?' he asked absently, studying the way that the sun caught the soft, downy hair of her body and blurred the warm voluptuous outline of curves and hollows.

'With a man. So . . . nice . . . fun.'

'*Nice?* Fun?' He was mock-affronted. 'What have I been doing wrong?'

'You know what I mean,' she said, refusing to allow him to tease her. She wanted him to know how wonderful he made her feel.

'I know.' He moved his body with remembered satisfaction, the brief togs hiding nothing of his powerful masculinity. 'You mean that we fit well together, that our enjoyment of each other isn't only physical.'

'Do you think . . . will it always be this good?'

His eyes narrowed, the irises expanding as he focused sharply on her face. 'What you you mean?'

'You know, sex,' she said hastily, not wanting him to think that she was implying anything he might take exception too, like commitment. She didn't want that either. 'Does it wear off? The . . . fun . . . the excitement? Is it just because it's new that I feel like this? Sort of high all the time. Leo?' She stared at him, disappointed, thinking he must have fallen asleep, his face was so still, his lashes quiet against the hard cheekbones. She felt foolish, not quite knowing what she was really asking, or why.

His eyes opened slowly. 'Are you afraid that *you'll* get bored in the bedroom, Gina?'

'N . . . no,' she wavered, misliking the very blandness of his expression. 'I just wondered.'

'Well, don't.' His eyes closed again. 'There's a time and a place, and this isn't it.'

'It' was much later on, in his bedroom, after a very frustrating and uncomfortable wrestle with the type-writer. It wasn't that Leo did anything out of the ordinary, but his silently reading figure seemed to radiate a kind of dangerous electrical aura that set Gina's skin prickling all over. The tingle seemed to settle along the insides of her thighs and the tips of her breasts and after resolutely trying to ignore it, Gina gave up.

'Leo, I'm not having much luck here. What say we give it a rest? I'll do extra tomorrow night, I promise.'

'Suits me.' He finished the last few paragraphs on the page he was reading and stood up to place it on the pile on the desk. While Gina packed up, he sauntered over to the bed and lay down on it, the dark wine shirt and cream trousers moulding the muscularity of his body.

The prickling intensified. When Gina had finished clearing the desk she stood uncertainly eyeing him.

'Switch off the lamp.'

Gina did as she was told, leaving the only light in the room the one beside the bed.

'Take your clothes off.'

Gina's breath caught in her lungs at the lazy command. 'Leo——'

'All of them. Take them off.'

Gina's mouth went dry and her palms began to sweat lightly, but she obeyed, her hands trembling as she removed her light, cool garments while he lay and watched, lounging indolently on the bed like a sultan inspecting one of his slave-girls. When at last she stood naked, her skin blooming with a dull sheen in the lamplight, he lifted a hand and beckoned.

'Come here.' His eyelids drooped to conceal the leaping fire in his eyes as again she obeyed without a word, moving towards him with the sensual grace that always succeeded in arousing him. He could see the excitement in her darkening eyes, the sexual curiosity stirring, lifting her gorgeous breasts, tightening her stomach. He rose to meet her and stood, not taking her into his arms, just making her wait.

Then, when she thought she would die from the waiting, he touched her, his hands moving across her skin, stroking her lightly. Occasionally he would dip his head and his mouth would brush hers but he drew away before she could fully taste his spicy warmth. She felt weak and shivery as she submitted to his leisurely appraisal but something held her back from moving, from breaking the incredibly exciting spell of sexual magnetism. Then he knelt and put his mouth to the heart of her feminine desire and she gasped and sagged over him, her eyes tightly closed as her hands wound themselves into the soft fabric across his shoulders. Suddenly his sweetly lashing tongue was gone and Gina opened her eyes, swaying, to see him standing before her, breathing fast, eyes glittering fiercely but face otherwise seemingly unmoved.

'Leo?' The stark, pleading whisper broke from bitten lips.

'Yes, Gina?' The crushed satin reply caressed her exposed nerves.

'W . . . what are you doing?'

His eyelids flicked back and yellow flame licked out at her. He raised a hand and splayed it between her breasts so that the tips of his fingers dug into the rounded flesh on either side.

'Making sure you don't get bored.'

He shoved violently so that Gina fell backwards on to the bed, her legs dangling over the edge, feet brushing the floor. She hardly had time to draw a startled breath before he was on her, mouth and hands full of savage demand, pulling open his clothing with careless strength as he ground himself against her. She moaned and he grasped her knees and pulled them up with a jerk, leaning over her and thrusting into her with a force that sent her heart slamming through the wall of her chest.

'Am I boring you, Gina?' he demanded hoarsely, lowering his mouth to her rigidly quivering breasts as his hands slid around the backs of her thighs, lifting her even more tightly against him so that he could plunge deeper into her velvet heat.

'No . . . no,' Gina gasped wildly, sweat beginning to glisten over her face and shoulders as the grinding sweetness began to wreak devastating havoc on her senses, sucking her into a whirlpool of pleasure such as she had never felt before.

He increased the aggressive tempo of his thrusts, bracing his knees against the bed to counterbalance each driving movement of his hips, taunting her over and over with the same hoarse demand until she was nearly screaming her reply.

'No . . . no . . . oh, please, Leo, don't stop . . . don't ever stop . . .' And he urged her on into ever wilder pleas until as last she shattered into a million tiny pieces in his arms, to be re-embodied by his own guttural groan of triumphant release.

'Oh, Leo . . .' she was sobbing in his arms and he was holding her half-laughing, half-groaning.

'Don't, Gina, don't cry. Ssshhh, it's all right now, you're back on the ground.' He pulled her up and round and fell beside her on the bed and she clutched at him.

'Are you sure?' She lifted her head and let it fall back again. 'My God, you didn't even take off your shoes!'

'Nor I did.' He twisted his body up to do so now, peeling off the rest of his clothing as well, and dropping it beside the bed, laughing at her incredulous expression. He held her close, absorbing the gentle after-shocks that quaked through her. 'I trust I put your mind to rest about us becoming bored with each other.'

'Yes ... yes, I think you did,' mumbled Gina, still dazed with wonder.

'Enough to persuade you to stay on?'

'I thought that's what I was doing.'

'I meant on a more permanent basis. Nic and I only have another month left here, will you keep us company?'

'And ... after ...?' Gina asked cautiously, afraid to press him but needing to get it straight in her mind exactly what he was offering.

'And after, too, if you'll have us.'

'You mean ... marriage?' She watched him carefully but he didn't pull back in horror. He looked ... satisfied, as if her cautious boldness pleased him.

'Eventually, yes, when you're more sure about me. No.' He pressed a finger against her lips. 'Don't talk any more about it now. I know that you're young and a little confused about your life right now. Let it ride for a while. We'll talk about it, and other things, again soon.'

Out of sheer exhaustion. Gina obeyed him yet again, but when she finally found her way back to her own bed she knew what her answer was going to be: Yes. She wasn't sure yet whether it was love she felt for Leo, having been proved wrong before on the subject, but she was fairly sure that what she did feel would move from strength to strength. Leo hadn't actually mentioned love but he didn't need to, he wouldn't mention marriage for any other reason—he didn't have to, she ruefully admitted. Doubtless that was one of the 'other things' he wanted to talk to her about.

The next morning she woke early and flew through her toilet and vocal exercises, anxious not to waste a single minute of the rest of her life. She had a coffee in the kitchen with Liana, who told her that Nic and his father had gone off to catch some fish for breakfast. As Gina finished her cup, which tasted extra flavoursome this beautiful morning, they heard the sound of engines overhead and Liana frowned.

'Did Mr Sterne say anything about the jet coming in? It can't be supplies, they came by boat yesterday.'

Gina shook her head. 'I'll go down and see, if you like.' She grinned. 'Better not disturb the fishermen at work.'

She had not the slightest inkling of disaster as she breathed in the warm, fragrant, sea-salted air as she approached the airstrip. She raised a hand to shade her eyes from the brilliantly-angled morning sun and frowned in puzzlement at the tall, elegantly thin brunette who moved confidently towards her, followed by the Lear jet's steward carrying two suitcases.

'Hello, you're not Miss Hamilton,' the woman commented, quite stunningly beautiful at close quarters. 'You must be the woman who thinks she can take my place. I'm Cynthia Sterne. I'm Leo's wife.'

'Ex-wife,' Gina found herself correcting numbly. Had Leo known she was coming? And how had she known about Gina?

The astonished laugh cut through her numbness like a knife. '*Ex*-wife? Is that what he told you? Poor you. We are still very married, my dear, and likely to stay that way if I know my Leo.'

CHAPTER TEN

EVEN now, three months later, Gina could vividly remember the bright unreality of that moment. It was crystallised forever as the single most shattering moment of her life, surpassing even the time she listened to the whey-faced doctor telling her that she no longer had a voice. The air had been sharp and painfully clear, the heat beginning to radiate up from the black tarmac as the morning fulfilled its promise of being another glorious day. And standing out from everything else was the image of Cynthia Sterne, as beautiful as Gina had imagined her to be—cool, composed, her eyes masked by dark glasses that emphasised her beauty.

Gina shivered in spite of the brightly burning fire warming the spacious room. She stared out of the floor-length window at the dark mass of cloud boiling up over the late-afternoon horizon. It was going to rain soon, heavily. There would be no sunset this evening, to draw her out of her sombre mood.

She knew what had prompted it. The oblong box lay on the desk in her studio. The galley proofs of *The Long Silence*. She had left the manuscript when she was driven from Paradise, too distraught to think of anything but escape. The unfinished work had turned up in the mail a few weeks later, without an accompanying letter. But she hadn't really expected one. What was there left to say? All the futile words had been said.

Gina stared rigidly out of the window, her eyes reflecting the stormy blackness of the clouds. Daniel had thought she was mad to buy this place, on an isolated section of Auckland's wind-swept west coast.

'It's designed to be a holiday residence, not for round-the-year occupation,' he protested. 'Besides, it's hours away from Auckland. What if I need you for a meeting?'

'It's scarcely the back of beyond,' Gina had said firmly, 'just because it hasn't got a telephone. If you want me urgently you can send a message to the post office. And I'll come into the city on a regular basis. I need the space, Daniel, at least for a while.'

'Are you *sure* you're over that bastard?' he demanded gruffly.

'I'm sure,' Gina smiled at him calmly. Daniel was way out of date but she had no intention of enlightening him as to her latest, more devastating, romantic disaster. Perhaps she was one of those women doomed to limp from one tragic love affair to the next.

Yet she knew, as she turned a deaf ear to her mother's aggrieved protests and shifted into her new home, that the description didn't really fit. She hadn't had an affair with Niven and it hadn't really been love. Gratitude, physical infatuation—a combination of many things, but not love. Love had been Leo and it had been an impossible one from the beginning, only she hadn't known it. Leo had withheld that knowledge deliberately, to protect her. He had been wrong but Gina was now mature enough to understand his motives. There was no question of forgiveness for she couldn't summon the heart to hate him, or even blame him. This time he had been as much a victim as she and in *extremis* had given her the final proof of his love—he had let her go when she begged him to, even though they both knew that he could have kept her, merely by taking her in his arms.

Gina had followed Cynthia Sterne back down to the villa and it was there in the lovely, light-filled lounge after despatching a stunned Liana to unpack her suitcase, that Leo's wife laid out her cards, one by one: a royal flush.

'I never did like it here very much—all those insects, and the sand gets everywhere.' Cynthia dismissed her surroundings with a shrug. 'Still, I suppose I can put up with it for a while for Nic's sake ... and Leo's, of course.'

'You're staying?' said Gina stupidly, when that much was obvious.

'Of course. It is half mine you know ... property acquired during the marriage.' The glasses were removed, revealing light-brown eyes that glittered, giving the lie to her coolness. There was a tightness to the lovely mouth that also warned Gina that although the woman spoke lightly there was a steely purpose behind her words.

'But ... you're separated.'

'And that's all we are, separated. Not divorced. Leo can't marry anyone else. That's what he likes about our little arrangement. It gives him an out against all the women who throw themselves at him.'

'He asked *me* to marry him,' Gina picked up the gauntlet hoarsely, trying not to let the pain show, the razor-sharp insult to slice away the trust that she had instinctively given Leo, along with her body. *He was married. He hadn't told her*. It danced, the old refrain.

'Did he say he loved you?'

'*Yes!*' But the lie only seemed to give the older woman more confidence.

'Then you won't be afraid to let him choose.'

'Choose?' Gina asked thickly, trying to blot out what she sensed was coming.

'Between you and his son!' A triumphant flush tinged Cynthia Sterne's fashionably hollow cheekbones.

'Nic ...?' Gina felt sick, her hand going to the throat. The brown eyes followed the gesture and narrowed with distaste at the sight of the scars. But the scent of blood was too strong to divert her from her purpose.

'Dominic! *My* son,' she spat. 'I raised him for six years with precious little help from your lover. Oh yes, I know you're sleeping together, I can read the signs and Leo was never one to curb his animal urges.' Her small fastidious shudder was revealing. Her husband's healthy sexuality had not fitted in, either, with her ideal of marriage. 'But just because you entertain him in bed doesn't make you indispensable in his life, not now he's suddenly decided that he wants Dominic. I'm not going to have my son brought up by anyone else. He needs his *real* mother, not some infatuated fool who's trying to get her greedy hooks into his father.'

'What are you going to do?' whispered Gina, afraid of the taut mask.

'Why, nothing.' The smile was horribly pleasant. 'I won't have to. No judge in the world would hand Dominic over to Leo on the evidence so far. Do you know, during all those years, he got his *secretary* to buy Christmas and birthday presents for Dominic? What kind of father does that? Oh no, if Leo thinks he can have it all his way he's mistaken. He can have you or Dominic, but not both. And if you're thinking to settle for being his live-in mistress, forget it. I didn't set the right moral tone for Dominic all these years just to have your lusts flaunted in his face!'

The coolness was slipping badly yet the woman was still speaking in a soft, well-modulated voice that would have graced any drawing-room. And, Gina realised, she hadn't come all this way to issue idle threats. She meant every word. And not because of Nic—she seemed to have conveniently forgotten all her own problems with Nic—no, she was bitter about how it would *look*. What people would say about the demise of the perfect marriage. About what they would think of a woman who gave up her son to her husband and a stranger to raise on their own.

'I would never hurt Nic,' she began roughly.

'But you'd take his father away from him, *if* Leo chose you. But you know he won't, don't you?' Her voice became kind as Gina's face registered stricken defeat. 'If you love him you won't force him to make that decision. It's for the best, you know. Because which ever way he went, in the end he would hate you for it. He would blame me; but hate you. The jet is going straight back to Auckland as soon as the pilot has done some checks and re-fuelled. Why don't you be on it? Leave Leo in peace with his son. That's all he really wants now, you know, his son.'

Gina had known in that blinding instant that she loved Leo more than anything else in the world. And regardless of his lies, and his cruel deception, she could not, would not put him through the torment of losing Nic, whom he had so recently found again, who was such a vulnerable part of him.

It took her only minutes to pack her bag. She brushed past Liana in the hall, not seeing her half-frightened look at the ashen-paleness of her skin, or noticing her run out towards the beach-track.

The pilot had finished re-fuelling. That ghastly scene with Cynthia Sterne must have consumed a whole half-hour, though at the time it had seemed quick and merciless. As he began checking the exterior of the plane Gina handed her single suitcase to the steward, who told her he had been expecting a return passenger, and turned to take one last look at Paradise.

She saw him striding up the embankment that levelled off the short runway and coming towards her with threatening swiftness, the sun glancing off his hair, making it look like the halo of some avenging angel. Gina was unable to move, her tongue cleaving to the roof of her mouth as he neared and she could see the sweat darkening his T-shirt, and the rigidity of his face.

He must have run from the beach. He was breathing heavily through his mouth and her name came out on a tortured breath. 'Gina!'

'I'm leaving.'

'Oh, God.' He dashed away the sweat that blurred his vision with an unsteady hand trying to summon control out of blind fear. 'Liana said—I had no idea . . . what has that bitch said to you?'

'Something that you should have said, long ago,' Gina hissed bitterly.

'I was going to——'

'When? Before you committed bigamy or after!'

'Gina, please.' He reached out but she knocked his hand away.

'Don't speak to me! Why should I listen to your lies! *Those* lies. I've heard them all before, remember?'

'At first . . . I had no intention . . .' he cursed at the unaccustomed lack of fluency when he most needed it. 'I didn't know that I was going to fall in love with you—it didn't start out that way. And then it was too late to tell you. Too late and too soon. We were lovers but you still didn't trust me. If you'd known you would have wanted to run away from me.'

'And I would have been right, wouldn't I?' she cried.

'It was selfish, I know, but I love you.'

She hated him with her eyes. 'Oh, yes, you can say that now, can't you, because I know you're married. Am I supposed to fall back in your arms and say that now we're lovers we may as well continue the adultery?'

Her scorn flayed his raw awareness of his own culpability. 'It's only adultery in the legal sense. Cynthia and I have lived strictly apart for years, both physically and emotionally.'

'So why are you still married?' she accused wildly.

'Because up until now there was no reason not to be. Neither of us wanted to get married again, and there were practical complications. During our marriage I quadrupled my assets and for tax reasons Cynthia has all sorts of interests in my various companies and investments. Rather than face the hassle of sorting it all out I let sleeping dogs lie.'

It made a weird kind of sense that Gina didn't want to understand.

'So if things are so nice and tidy between you, what's

she doing here now, defending her unoccupied territory?' she confronted him fiercely.

'Because her feelings about Nic aren't so neat and tidy, and she's probably just received the divorce papers.'

She had just found out about his marriage . . . now it was *divorce*? Gina staggered back against the hot metal of the side of the plane.

'I wanted to set the wheels in motion before I told you, as an act of faith,' he said intensely, following up the advantage. 'Trust me, Gina, I can handle whatever it is she wants, just give me time.'

'Nic . . . she wants Nic,' Gina whispered, the tears on her cheeks. 'She means to make you choose.'

'No!' His face was milked suddenly of its colour, the golden eyes opaquely registering the blow, rejection, revulsion.

'She's going to take him away if I don't go,' she sobbed.

'She won't do it. She's temporarily insane . . . it's bluff,' he said with a savagery that rent Gina's heart with agony.

'She can do it, though, Leo, can't she?' Gina tortured herself. 'Are you willing to take that chance on Nic's future? On losing him?'

'I love you.' He smashed his fist brutally into the hard metal against which Gina leaned, as if he could smash down this new, insurmountable barrier to their happiness. 'I won't let her.' He turned his face to her, bloodied but unbeaten. 'Tell me you love me, Gina. Tell me that at least. My God, if a cynical bastard like me can believe in love why the hell can't you?'

'I believe,' she whispered, weakened by her need, but fighting it for his sake, 'I love you. But that's all I can give you, the words. I can't stay, please don't make my love a burden.'

'Gina.' He turned her into the side of the plane and forced the words back into her mouth with his. He kissed her with savagery, devouring her tears, swallowing them as if he would swallow her and keep her hidden in a secret place inside where no one else could reach, where no one else would be able to hurt or hold her. Gina wound her arms around him and kissed him back with equal fervour, revelling in the way that the muscled wall of his chest flattened her woman's breasts and the hot pulse of his loins impressed her with his raging desire. And she wanted to stay there forever.

'Don't cry, darling, I promise I'll——'

'No!' Gina tore herself out of his embrace, her hand against her mouth to hold in the words of pain. 'No promises, Leo. No lies. Just let me go. Don't make me want to stay, don't make me hate myself . . . please, if you really do love me . . .'

Her last sight of him was standing on the deserted runway below, the breeze ruffling the bright gold of his hair, his head thrown back, stance stiff, filled with the agony of defeat. Her wild and wondrous magician with all his spells broken, his power usurped.

It was a picture that she carried in her heart, along with the irony that she had not lost him because he loved too little, but because he loved too much. How could she hate him for loving Nic? Gina loved him too, and not just for being Leo's son, and it hurt to have him thinking badly of her because she had not said goodbye. But it was better than having involved him in an ugly, three-way tug-of-war. Perhaps, one day, he would be able to understand, and forgive.

Gina dragged herself back to the present, rubbing her arms through the fleecy mohair sweater which matched her blue stirrup cords. No use dwelling on the past, it made her too frighteningly aware of the hollowness of the present, and the fragility of the life that she was rebuilding yet again. If only she could stop feeling so cold . . . and it had nothing to do with the weather.

She made herself an omelette for supper, aware that she was eating too many eggs because they were quick and easy to prepare, and less of a hardship on a stomach which tended to churn up when she contemplated the idea of a lifetime without Leo. She was still learning to cook, after always having had servants at home, and was finding that independence had disadvantages as well as blessed freedoms. Being able to work whenever she liked and enjoy casual, erratic mealtimes was a bonus that was reflected in her work. Daniel was pleased with her at the moment, particularly with the dogged work she had done on *The Long Silence*. Without Leo to goad and encourage it had been a struggle, but she was grimly proud of the result. Had he read it? she wondered. Was he proud of her, or disappointed? She longed to know, aware that much of her longing stemmed from the desire just to see him, to speak to him again whatever the long-term pain involved.

Stoking up the fire Gina prepared to settle with a book as she listened to the wind boom against the low cliff on which the row of beach houses was perched. Each house was divided into two, the other half of Gina's owned by a retired businessman who, like most of the other residents, only visited when the weather was favourable.

The solitary situation suited Gina's current frame of mind. Winter suited her: the stark trees, the bitter weather, the turbulence of sea and sky that reflected the turbulence inside her. Although she thought often of Leo she tried not to wonder too much if he was as alone, as lonely, as she was. He had Nic but Nic was a boy. Desolately Gina believed that when Leo finally accepted that he couldn't have what he wanted he would put his love behind him, ruthlessly, and go on. He would realise that the quick, clean break was for the best. He would become the Magician again—powerful, in control, and go on to weave his spells around other women. He might even fall in love again some time in the future, when Nic was more mature. Gina might fall in love, too, but it would never be the same. Something in her had died when she had made that unwilling sacrifice. If she ever met a man with whom she felt she could make a life, he wouldn't be in any way like Leo. She couldn't bear that. She would want someone quiet of spirit with whom she could be at peace. There had been too many violent emotions in her life and she wanted no more of them. Better to be lonely than to try to imitate what had been so preciously unique about her first love ... she would become twisted and bitter at each failure and she wanted no bitterness to mar her memories.

She was so engrossed in her book that when the knock came she got up and almost opened the door before she remembered where she was. Her hand froze on the door handle. Who could it be in this isolated spot? The rutted road that led up here was a private one that finished in a dead-end, so there were never any casual passers-by. Had one of the other owners misplaced a key? At this hour, in this weather?

'Who is it?' she asked, hoping her deep voice might persuade the person outside that there was a man in residence.

'Leo. Open up, Gina.'

It must be the wind, playing tricks on her. There wasn't anyone out there at all.

'Gina, come on, open this door.'

Gina's hand was glued to the handle, but she didn't dare turn it. The voice was stomach-wrenchingly familiar but it was only a projection from her mind. Had she been going mad and not realised it? Playing games with herself? All that rubbish about falling in love again, when deep down she despaired that she ever would? And being happy for Leo, when jealousy burnt like acid inside her at the thought of him even being able to *exist* without her? When in the back of her mind were microscopic seeds of anger and resentment that she had had to make the decision she did. She could have been his secret mistress, couldn't she? If he had loved her so madly why hadn't he suggested it? Horrified by these ugly, alien thoughts that had sprung out of her fear, Gina sagged against the door.

'Go away, I don't want you,' she sobbed hoarsely, to the sickness in her mind, the phantom in the dark. Silence. Madness after all.

'I can't go away. My car is stuck in that bloody bog you call a road!' That prosaic blend of grim humour and impatient anger hadn't come from any phantom. Gina unlocked her muscles and opened the door a crack. Immediately a muddy shoe rammed into the breach. 'Let me in.' And at her frighted look, 'For God's sake stop staring at me as if I'm some roaming sex fiend.' His mouth twisted. 'Sex fiend I may be, but roaming I'm not.'

'You're wet,' whispered Gina blankly, not hearing him, just devouring the sight of him. He wasn't wearing a coat, only a black sweater and slacks and his face looked pale against the dark, wet wool. Apart from the paleness he looked the same as ever, as if he hadn't suffered a single iota.

'It's raining,' he pointed out, as another drenching gust of wind flung wetness at him. Seeing that she was in some kind of huge-eyed trance he took the initiative and shoved his way inside, going straight over to the fire, stretching white-knuckled hands out to its heat.

Gina followed him jerkily, her heart pounding. 'What are you doing here?' she croaked, afraid of the answer.

'Well, I didn't come up here for the scenery,' he mocked tightly, turning to study her shock, noting her slenderness and the inner tension that showed in the finely drawn features. She looked tired, lost. She had probably been working too hard, busy being brave in this nun-like retreat. He trembled at the thought of what he intended to do to her after they had talked and the way she would respond, had always responded to him. She misinterpreted his shiver and he felt a sting of triumph as he saw her shock melt into concern: so she still loved him, she didn't hate him for what he had put her through.

'You must be cold as ice, you'd better get dry,' Gina said stiffly, trying to behave as if she didn't want to wrap her arms around him and warm him with the heat of her own body.

'Later——'

'But——'

'Don't mother me, Gina.' He wiped the rain off his face with his arm and slicked back his wet hair. 'I didn't come here looking for a mother—for me, or for Nic.'

'Then why?' Why was he tormenting her with his presence if nothing had changed? Was he going to offer her second best, *now*, when she could very easily hate him for too little, too late?

'A friend . . .' *Friendship!* Was he so insensitive? '. . . a lover . . .' Oh, *God*! '. . . a wife . . .'

The last crippled her breath. 'Leo . . .?'

'I'm divorced.'

'No!' She swayed, blood singing in her ears, swelling in her throat, locking off her reason. A trick, a lie. It was too much to hope for, so she hadn't let herself. Had played the game of acceptance . . .

'I got the final papers today. I brought them with me. I'm not asking you to believe me this time, Gina, I've brought the proof.' He said it quietly, evenly, as if he knew any emotion at this point would push her over the edge. He reached inside the crew-neck of his damp sweater and drew out a long, thick white envelope and held it out to her.

She shook her head. 'I don't want to see, I don't want to see.' Her eyes lifted to his; almond windows of pain and something else—the beginnings of a terrible hope.

'See that I still love you, want to marry you? I never stopped loving or wanting. *God*, how I wanted!' The last slipped out involuntarily.

'Nic?'

'Is mine, to bring up how and with whom I choose. Ours, darling.'

'But Cynthia?' She staved off the moment she would go to him, prolonging the agonising wait for pleasure as Leo had often done when they were making love.

The envelope fluttered to the floor, unnoticed.

'She's getting married again, too.' His mouth twisted at her incredulous stare. 'Someone more her type—very polished, fastidious, not to mention gentlemanly—he asked her months ago and it had been preying on her mind ... he's not too keen on children apparently. But she couldn't bring herself to relinquish Nic entirely and felt guilty about wanting to. I guess when I gave her the perfect out she refused to face it. Of course, once you left and she found she had what she wanted she realised she didn't want it any more. With one or two hiccups we managed to settle our affairs with a minimum of animosity. Mind you, it was touch and go whether I murdered her back on Paradise. You have Thomas and Liana to thank that I'm not behind bars.'

'I didn't think you could get a divorce so quickly,' said Gina. Quickly? It had seemed like aeons since they had last held each other in that desperate embrace.

'We'd been separated so long it was only a matter of formality. What took the time was working out terms about Nic and sorting out the financial tangles.'

The implication of his words shattered the last barriers of Gina's restraint. She came to life, a cold statue flooding with colour, with love and rage so forcefully intermingled they were indivisible.

'Do you mean to tell me,' she stormed at him wildly, body quivering with outrage, 'that you've known for weeks, *months*, that you were going to be free and you never bothered to let me know? You *love*! Yet you abandoned me and left me to, to ...' she choked helplessly on her fury, and struck out as Leo moved swiftly, pulling her against him. He held her hard by the shoulders and shook her.

'I didn't dare. If I had let myself see you, or even speak to you or tried to put it into words on paper I would have lost control. I'm like an alcoholic ... the sight and sound and touch and feel of you, even the thought of you sets up an uncontrollable craving. But having you with me might have only have jeopardised everything. It was touch and go with Cynthia at times, she really is the most contrary bitch, and it wouldn't have been fair to set you up as a target, you're too vulnerable to her kind of poison. Besides, it was you who abandoned *me*, remember? Daniel Austin told me that you'd moved up here and I was terrified you were hiding yourself away from me, hating me. I had to make up for those lies, Gina, for giving you reason to mistrust me. When I came to you again I wanted it to be free and clear. This time I wanted it to be——'

'Perfect.' She had stopped fighting him at his first words, feeding on the wry, self-derisive confession, loving him for his stupidity. 'Oh, Leo, weren't you the one who told me that nothing and no one is perfect?'

The husky indulgence in her voice was like the striking of a match in the dark of his soul. 'You still love me.'

'I still sleep with you every night.'

'God.' He groaned, hands sliding around her back, moving down to her waist, and lower, grinding her hips against his. He smelt of wet wool and male desire and already she could feel the hardness between his thighs, and the softening between hers. 'I missed you, Nic missed you—I couldn't tell him either. At first he punished me by saying he wanted to go and live with his mother but after a lot of yelling and crying he changed his mind.'

'He cried over me?' Nic ... who had tantrums but rarely cried?

'We both did,' he nuzzled away the hair from the side of her neck and bit her, and licked the wound. 'I suspect he loved every moment of it, seeing big, bad

Daddy crying. When you sent us that book he made me read it to him every night in bed. I think we're raising a little sadist.'

'I'm sorry.' She had sent Leo an advance copy of *Jao and the Magician*, not daring to risk upsetting Nic by addressing it to him. Like Leo she had written no note, having too much, and nothing, to say.

'Don't be, it did us both good to share a sorrow. Am I still *your* Magician, Gina?' His hand traced the sideseam of her skin-tight cords and slipped around to cup her boldly between the legs, fingers stroking against her heat.

'Yes, oh yes.' She arched greedily against him, allowing him access. 'Please, show me some magic, some of your special magic.'

He tore off his clothes and hers while they stood there; licking, sucking, biting at her succulent flesh before pulling her down to the carpet and drinking in her cries and whispers as he parted the secret of her female flesh and explored her with his fingers, his eyes, his mouth. At last, when he had driven them both to the limits of endurance, when he saw that Gina could not speak, could only mouth her impassioned pleas, he gave a strange and wild laugh and completed their union with a single violent stroke that impaled her body, her heart, her brain on his iron-hard desire. She climaxed on the instant and he so quickly afterwards that they stared at each other, bemused, both panting, still locked together, sated yet regretful.

'I'm sorry,' he growled, rolling her over with his sweat-slick body so that her back was warmed by the fire. 'It's been so long ... I meant to hold back but I couldn't.'

Nor could I, Gina mimed and he gave a husky chuckle.

'I'm so glad that I still send you speechless.' He kissed her mouth with a gentleness that cherished. 'I seem to have wanted you forever. Even, God forgive me, with my sister crying in my arms, you got to me. That's why I was so furious when you turned up on Paradise. I loathed myself for wanting you and was outraged that my son preferred you to me. I told myself I wanted to keep you on the island to help Nic, but my reasons were far more complex. As I began to find out more about you I began to discover my own duplicity. I began to feel protective towards you and I've never felt that about a women before . . . even Cynthia. It played merry hell with my other needs . . . I *had* to find out what it was about you that drove me so crazy. Finding out you were a virgin didn't stop me wanting to seduce you, it only excited me more, and I appeased what little conscience I had by that stage by telling myself that you needed a real lover to help you get over Niven.'

'I think I did,' Gina confessed, amused, delighted, and flattered by his depiction of his confused state of mind . . . every bit as confused as her own had been. 'But it also made me wonder if I knew what real love was, if I would be able to recognise it when it happened. I knew what I felt for you was strong, special, but I wasn't sure if it was love.'

'I know, that's what kept me from forcing the pace, even though I was sure that you were falling in love with me,' he told her, looking lovingly into her blissful face. 'I was certain that I was in love with you the first time we went to bed together. You know I've had other lovers, but none of them turned me inside out the way you did, just by *being*. You had no tricks, no artifice, and yet ecstasy was easy with you. Your fate was sealed then and there, I didn't want to ever let you go but I knew I had to go easy. I was afraid of frightening you off by telling you how I felt, and I was even more frightened of telling you that I was still married. It was bloody silly, in retrospect, but I thought I could spare you that and only ended up hurting you more instead. Letting you leave that day was the hardest thing I've ever done, but I thought

Harlequin Presents

Coming Next Month

943 ISHBEL'S PARTY Stacy Absalom
A peaceful Suffolk village seems the perfect place for a nurse to recover from injuries, but for the presence of the man she lost that awful night of Ishbel's party—the man she still loves.

944 THE PUPPET MASTER Pippa Clarke
The man who's trying to close down her sister's Mediterranean restaurant might be the puppet master, but Anna is no willing marionette. Still, seeing him with his ex-lover does tug at her heartstrings.

945 ADAM'S LAW Claudia Jameson
A domineering sculptor tries to bully an injured model back to life, back to her glamorous career in the city. But she'd miss life in Guernsey and the love she's found there.

946 DESIRE NEVER CHANGES Penny Jordan
The daughter of a British ambassador is shocked when a world-renowned photographer threatens to expose compromising photos he took of her five years ago—unless she agrees to marry him!

947 IMPACT Madeleine Ker
A young woman meeting her fiancé's best friend for the first time is confused when he tries to turn her against the man she's promised to marry—especially since she knows he's right.

948 BODYCHECK Elizabeth Oldfield
Attraction flares between a model and her bodyguard in Paris. Yet she's afraid to break things off with her boyfriend, even though she appears to be a "good-time girl" dangling two men on the line.

949 ELUSIVE PARADISE Lilian Peake
"Who'll be prince to my Cinderella?" a researcher asks at her friend's wedding reception, never expecting her new boss to answer in earnest. Why, his reputation for dealing ruthlessly with staff is legend.

950 TIME FOR ANOTHER DREAM Karen van der Zee
Indecision plagues a young widow after she convinces the head of a sheltered workshop in Virginia that she isn't a flighty socialite. Her thoughts about her new boss have definitely turned to fancy.

Available in January wherever paperback books are sold, or through Harlequin Reader Service:

In the U.S.
P.O. Box 1397
Buffalo, N.Y.
14240-1397

In Canada
P.O. Box 603
Fort Erie, Ontario
L2A 9Z9

ATTRACTIVE, SPACE SAVING BOOK RACK

Display your most prized novels on this handsome and sturdy book rack. The hand-rubbed walnut finish will blend into your library decor with quiet elegance, providing a practical organizer for your favorite hard-or soft-covered books.

Only $9.95

Approximately 16" x 8" when assembled

Assembles in seconds!

To order, rush your name, address and zip code, along with a check or money order for $10.70 ($9.95 plus 75¢ postage and handling) (New York residents add appropriate sales tax), payable to *Harlequin Reader Service* to:

In the U.S.

Harlequin Reader Service
Book Rack Offer
901 Fuhrmann Blvd.
P.O. Box 1325
Buffalo, NY 14269-1325

Offer not available in Canada.

Can you keep a secret?

You can keep this one plus 4 free novels

A page-turning combination of romance, suspense and international intrigue!

TELL ME NO LIES

Lindsay Danner is the only one who can lead the search for the invaluable Chinese bronzes. Jacob Catlin is the only one who can protect her. They hadn't planned on falling in love....

ELIZABETH LOWELL

Six exciting series
for you every month...
from Harlequin

Harlequin Romance·
The series that started it all

Tender, captivating and heartwarming...
love stories that sweep you off to faraway places
and delight you with the magic of love.

♦

Harlequin Presents·
Powerful contemporary love
stories...as individual as the
women who read them

The No. 1 romance series...
exciting love stories for you, the woman of today...
a rare blend of passion and dramatic realism.

♦

Harlequin Superromance®
It's more than romance...
it's Harlequin Superromance

A sophisticated, contemporary romance-fiction
series, providing you with a longer,
more involving read...a richer mix of complex plots,
realism and adventure.

Harlequin American Romance™
Harlequin celebrates the American woman...

...by offering you romance stories written about American women, by American women for American women. This series offers you contemporary romances uniquely North American in flavor and appeal.

◆

Harlequin Temptation™
Passionate stories for today's woman

An exciting series of sensual, mature stories of love...dilemmas, choices, resolutions... all contemporary issues dealt with in a true-to-life fashion by some of your favorite authors.

◆

Harlequin Intrigue
Because romance can be quite an adventure

Harlequin Intrigue, an innovative series that blends the romance you expect... with the unexpected. Each story has an added element of intrigue that provides a new twist to the Harlequin tradition of romance excellence.

Harlequin Books·

PROD-A-2

Don't miss a single title from this great collection. The first eight titles have already been published. Complete and mail this coupon today to order books you may have missed.

Harlequin Reader Service

In U.S.A.
901 Fuhrmann Blvd.
P.O. Box 1397
Buffalo, N.Y. 14140

In Canada
P.O. Box 2800
Postal Station A
5170 Yonge Street
Willowdale, Ont. M2N 6J3

Please send me the following titles from the Janet Dailey Americana Collection. I am enclosing a check or money order for $2.75 for each book ordered, plus 75¢ for postage and handling.

_____	ALABAMA	Dangerous Masquerade
_____	ALASKA	Northern Magic
_____	ARIZONA	Sonora Sundown
_____	ARKANSAS	Valley of the Vapours
_____	CALIFORNIA	Fire and Ice
_____	COLORADO	After the Storm
_____	CONNECTICUT	Difficult Decision
_____	DELAWARE	The Matchmakers

Number of titles checked @ $2.75 each = $_____

N.Y. RESIDENTS ADD
   APPROPRIATE SALES TAX $_____

Postage and Handling $ _.75_

              TOTAL $_____

I enclose _____

(Please send check or money order. We cannot be responsible for cash sent through the mail.)

PLEASE PRINT

NAME _____

ADDRESS _____

CITY _____

STATE/PROV. _____